HOW
TO
STEAL
A GALAXY

HOW
TO
STEAL
A GALAXY

BETH REVIS

DAW BOOKS
NEW YORK

Jacket design by Adam Auerbach
Book design by Fine Design
Edited by Navah Wolfe
DAW Book Collectors No. 1973

DAW Books
An imprint of Astra Publishing House
dawbooks.com
DAW Books and its logo are registered trademarks of
Astra Publishing House

Printed in the United States of America

Library of Congress Cataloging-in-Publication Data

Names: Revis, Beth, author.
Title: How to steal a galaxy / Beth Revis.
Description: First edition. | New York : DAW Books, 2024. |
Series: Chaotic Orbits ; book 2
Identifiers: LCCN 2024034618 (print) | LCCN 2024034619 (ebook) |
ISBN 9780756419486 (hardcover) | ISBN 9780756419493 (ebook)
Subjects: LCGFT: Fantasy fiction. | Romance fiction. | Novels.
Classification: LCC PS3618.E895 H69 2024 (print) |
LCC PS3618.E895 (ebook) | DDC 813/.6--dc23/eng/20240801
LC record available at https://lccn.loc.gov/2024034618
LC ebook record available at https://lccn.loc.gov/2024034619

First edition: December 2024
10 9 8 7 6 5 4 3 2 1

DEDICATION

Dedicated to desperation,
a true soul-killer that almost did me in.
Almost. I survived, and now I'm going
to make that everyone's problem.

· ·

EPIGRAPH

In lieu of an actual epigraph, go to your local independent bookstore or library, find a copy of *Dream Work* by Mary Oliver, turn to the poem "Wild Geese," and read the first line of that poem.

1

I dock *Glory* in bay ninety-four at the outer Oort station and ping my contact. I know it won't take him long to get to me, but also I've had nothing but recycler worms for the entire journey away from the *Roundabout* wreckage, so I hop out. Stations always have a variety of food and people selling them, and this one is pretty big, with lots of cruiser transfers. I grab some skewers of something brown and crunchy as an appetizer—surprisingly sweet—and then get closer to the center, where the good stuff is.

My contact finds me bent over a cart, picking a flavor of a protein drink. "There you are," he says, his voice low and gruff. "Why did you leave the bay?"

"I'll take a purple one, with some of those cold cubes," I tell the vendor, pointing. "And he's paying."

The vendor bends into her cart, scooping out the squishy cubes into the reusable cup I hand her.

"No, I'm not," my contact says. I don't know his name. He told me once before, but eh. I ping him with the code word, and he shows up; that's all this ever needs to be.

"You are paying," I say, my voice betraying a bit of an edge. "Because I have your stuff. Want anything?" I grin at the vendor as I take the cup back.

Grudgingly, my contact taps his cuff against the vendor's scanner. "Come on," he growls, leading me back to *Glory*. When we're far enough away from others, he says in a low voice, "You got all three items we need?"

I slurp the purple drink. "Yup."

He frowns and looks like he wants to say more, but a group of people walks close by. I motion for him to follow me into the docking bay and on board the ship.

He looks around at my little *Glory* as if she wasn't the best ship in the entire galaxy, which says a lot about how bad his taste is. Even with a hole in her side that I have to seal off behind the bulkhead doors, *Glory*'s lovely.

"You have comms down, right?" he asks.

"Obviously," I snap. Everyone knows that all communication runs through the portal network, and the portal network is run by the government using the same system base. The law-abiding types tend to point out that comms are on private relays, but it doesn't take much figuring to guess that "private relays" are only private as long as no one wants to listen.

And there are a lot of people who want to listen to what my contact has to say.

"Speaking of security, you do know that the code word

Jane Irwin is, er, how shall I put this? Too well fucking known." I head toward the bridge, the contact on my heels.

"We know," he says.

I shoot him an exasperated look over my shoulder as I lean down to the bridge box and get out the data recorder that has all the information from the cryptex drive on it.

"It's a base code at best, and a way to recognize who may be working undercover. We let the law think they know the right code so they don't dig deeper, and we weed out some low-levels by using it." He looks down at the box as I hand it to him. "This is useless without the key and the prototype."

"Sure is. Just like you're useless until I see the payment in my account." I pointedly look at the data band on my wrist, already glowing with my financial info.

The contact heaves a sigh. "Some people would help us because it's the right thing to do," he says. "I am not getting paid. Knowing that I could save billions of people is payment enough, and—"

I clear my throat and tap my band.

His jaw works while he pulls out a data pad, punches a code on the screen, waits, taps a few more times. In moments, the sum we agreed upon flashes in my account.

"Wonderful!" I say brightly. I reach into my pocket for the small box that contains the cryptex key and the nanobot prototype and toss it to him.

He fumbles, dropping his data pad to catch the box. "Hey, this is sensitive material!"

"It's *fine,*" I say. "If that little nanobot is supposed to figure out a way to clean up the pollution on Earth, then it's going to have to take a bigger beating than just being tossed a few meters."

He stares down at the box as if it holds the answers to life, the universe, and everything.

Maybe it does.

No, who am I kidding. It just holds a key and bot.

"Any trouble?" he asks.

"Some," I say. I was already in place when *Roundabout* came into view. I watched as the crew inside evacuated and got picked up by another ship in my contact's network. I suppose there's some sort of cover for the crew. They were all Earthers; I know that much. Anyway, after the crew left, they set a crash course for *Roundabout* onto the terran protoplanet.

"You were *supposed* to crash the ship neater," I point out. The plan had been to wreck the *Roundabout,* then let me loot the goods the operation needed and be gone before anyone else showed up. It was the best plan to keep the crew alive and still get the data, and with the crash, there was an excellent chance it would be weeks before the government even knew the material was missing. With a freighter like that, any pause to open up a cofferdam or allow outside boarding would have sent immediate alarms through the system, and probably the United Galactic Systems Navy would show up, guns blazing. But by crashing the ship, communication was just cut off. No one would know about the evac crew until they saw the crash site. And the government agencies monitoring the *Roundabout* would believe they'd have to gather up a salvage crew, wasting valuable time.

Time that I could have spent getting the goods and getting out.

Had the ship's crash site not been quite so bad.

"We did what we could," the contact says. "And it can't have been *too* difficult. You got the stuff."

The crew of the *Roundabout* knew the drive was in the bridge box, and they suspected the key was in one of the cargo crates—but all the cargo crates had been linked to the security system, so they couldn't locate it before the wreck.

"It was a hassle, is what it was," I grumble. "I deserve a bonus. I have to pay for repairs that I incurred running *your* job. Which was also in the middle of fucking nowhere."

"You knew that going in."

I did. The *Roundabout's* course was set on an unusual path that was supposed to be off the charts. But it was heading to a nanobot factory on one of the little unnamed worlds with no atmosphere. Safer to produce something directly designed to interfere with water cycles on a world without water. If it malfunctions, you just scrap the design without risking ruining the whole freaking planet.

Bots are wild. I don't really mess with them, because I don't like the idea of someone programming something invisible to the naked eye that can mess you up. People used to use them for everything, including biological and medical issues, but some regs came out limiting their use. Thing is, bots work like a virus—they can replicate, and they can infect other bots with bad coding. No one volunteers these days to infect themselves with nanobots that a coder could bust into and hack your own *body*. But for things like the environment? I guess the government cleared that.

Infect a whole planet, see what happens.

My contact tilts his head back, looking down his nose at me as if he has me all figured out. "You're not in it just for the money."

"I am," I snap back immediately. "Also, did you not notice the hole in my hull? It's kind of big deal. And it's gonna cost a lot."

He starts shaking his head, this little smirk on his face really tempting me to just punch him. "Nah, you say it's about cash, but really? You care."

"Of course I *care*," I snarl. It was why I was willing to risk *Glory* to get the work done. "But if the *Halifax* had offered me more than you guys did, I would have taken it. Those people weren't even willing to give me seconds at mealtime."

"You interacted directly with the government salvage?" My contact is surprised.

"Mm," I say, looking at my data band to find a repair at the station.

"How much interaction did you—"

"I was on the *Halifax* for a few nights," I say. "And I would charge you overtime, but they fed me well. Except for being stingy with the portions." I take a moment and think about that chicken. That *peach*. I wonder how much luxury food costs on Rigel-Earth. Probably as much as this repair is going to cost.

"Did you—"

"I didn't learn anything you don't already know," I say, sighing as I look up at him. "Probably only the government operative on board knew the full picture of what they were salvaging."

"Who—"

"Rian White."

He leans back. "Oh."

A tone like that? My body goes still. "What's that *oh* mean?"

"We've run into White a few times. He's . . . observant."

Damn right he is.

"Won't take a bribe," he continues.

Not surprising.

My contact weighs the box in his hand. "He's an operative, not a decision-maker, but he's someone who influences those who do make the calls. But . . . White doesn't know coding."

And there's the rub. See, Rian wants to help Earth. But he believes there are proper channels for that, *official* ways to help. That the government arcs slowly but eventually bends toward goodwill. So, he probably headed a commission for solutions, and he probably listened to all sorts of private investors who came up with action plans, and then he probably helped pick the final companies to manufacture these nanobots that are supposed to clean up Earth.

Except he doesn't know code.

And these guys, my contact and his lot? They do. And they know that the company ultimately hired for the job isn't like Rian. They don't care about anything but profits.

Guess we have that in common.

"So, you made contact with White," my contact muses. "How did that go?"

I shrug. My eyes are on my data band. There's only one repair shop that can see me without a wait, but they're pricy as hell.

"Listen, all cards on the table," he continues, his voice beseeching me to look up. I don't. "We know that this data can be replicated by the government. At most, we've delayed their plans, not stopped them. And maybe we're wrong! Maybe when our people inspect the coding, we'll see nothing but what the government has said it's making—climate cleaners that are going to help fix Earth. Maybe it's all going to be fine."

He's wrong. I've already looked at the coding. It's designed to go bad. But he'll figure that out on his own, and I don't want him to know how much I know.

He sighs, making a show of running a hand through his shoulder length hair. "But," he continues, somehow even more serious, "maybe when we look at this code, maybe we find that there's some malware or something on these bots." Yup. "We're working on a time limit. Once these nanobots release, if they are designed to spy or hack or exploit the system . . . we're all fucked. All of Earth. A whole planet fucked. Microscopic bots programmed to alter the environment can't exactly be put back in the bottle once they're released, and if they have any type of malicious programming hidden inside their coding—"

I go ahead and book the expensive guy for the repairs. *Glory* can fly with that hole in her side, but it'd be better to patch her up. "You should be paying for this," I grumble.

"We will."

My head whips up.

"If," he adds, "you join the cause. Use bravado if you need to save face, but we hired you for a reason."

"Because I get the job done."

"Because you care."

By all the fucking stars out in the black, he's *smiling* now. My fingers curl into fists.

"You care about Earth; you care about the people of

Earth," he continues as if he's not spouting bullshit. "And you knew what this mission was for, and that's why you went as far as you did to get what we needed."

"Look, I have a competitive streak that is perhaps not healthy, I will give you that," I say, my voice pitched low enough to make him raise his eyebrows in surprise. "But do not try to entangle me in with your little schemes and subterfuge. I did the job. You paid me for the job. We're done."

"But if you have an in with White, and if this coding proves our theory that the bots are corrupt—"

"Then you can maybe hire me for another job," I say. "But my rates are going up. If I have to listen to you preach at me about *causes*, then I'm going to charge you an hourly."

He huffs a little, but I cross my arms and stare him down.

"Fine," he says finally, and he stomps out.

One Month Later

I'm wrapping up a different job—no need for details; it involved explosives but ended up quite boring overall—when I get a ping from the contact.

Suspicions confirmed. Code bad. Let's talk.

They're limiting what info they send, knowing comms

are never truly secure. I send back a number with a lot of zeroes at the end as my price.

They don't reply.

One Month After That

I'm kicking my heels up on the Zoozve base when I get another ping.

We need you.

I send back the same number.

We don't have those kinds of funds.

I send back a number higher than that.

It's a different mission. Undercover.

I tack on another ten thousand.

They counter with a much, much lower number—although a better one than they started with—and attach it to a message that reads: *This is all the funds we have for the job.*

I hesitate. I mean, sure, okay, there was a *little* bravado in how I spoke to the contact. I don't actually want Earth swarming with malicious nanobots just because the government's too inept to inspect the coding of the bots they buy. And it's been made patently obvious that none of the colonized worlds care about the old homestead, not enough to actually *do* anything.

I get another ping. *We need you to talk to Rian White.*

I stare at the glowing letters on my dash.

Fuck it.

I'm in.

2

The Museum of Intergalactic History glitters almost as much as I do. The hem of my dress swishes, catching light from the circle luminaries hovering next to the camera drones. I don't have the face of a celebrity—even though I absolutely grinned at every scanner on the way up the dramatic stairs—so none of the cams turn to capture my visage as I put one elegantly pointed silver shoe on the top step, my leg peeking through the decadent slit up the skirt as ripples of gossamer-like cloth flutter behind me. Not a single drone so much as twitches in my direction.

Which is a damn shame, because I look really hot. Especially in this light.

Rigel is a blue star system, unlike the yellow sun of Earth, and diamond hour is legit. Not only is the afternoon light casting lovely blue shadows over everything, but Rigel-Earth can see more than one star in the sky. The main star is a supergiant, but it's got a cluster of little sisters—four of them, all blue. This world is far enough away that Rigel doesn't look that much bigger from the surface of the planet than the Sun looks from Earth, despite being something like twenty times larger, and the sister stars aren't always visible to the naked eye. But twilight lasts longer, the glow extending for hours, and the sunrise—if you're awake for that sort of thing—is almost worth putting up with the people on this planet for.

Almost.

The diamond-hour glow highlights the museum's portico, the sculpture in the pediment angled to catch the dying light—a giant of a man, kneeling, a sword at his belt hanging down over the entrance, a bow pointed up in a way that, supposedly, lines up with the main star at the equinox. This is a bronzed version of Orion, the constellation Rigel is in, and sure enough, the foot on the right is wearing a shoe enhanced with some glittering blue gem, symbolizing the star.

So fucking pretentious, honestly.

The landing under the portico is marred by a series of scanners, and there's a little bit of a wait to get inside. Everything here is still pretty mild, but it's going to get chaotic fast. Part of me wants to revel in the whirlwind I know is coming in the next half hour or so as the celebrities, politicians, and generally famous-for-being-famous people arrive. But the more sensible part of me knows I need to focus. Get inside, start laying the groundwork. And this sort of party always has good food, so that'll be nice.

I'm arriving unfashionably early. But what was I going

to do, sit in *Glory* and while away the minutes in the docking bay? Not a chance. What I want is inside that building.

One goal. Full speed.

I don't even bother biting back the grin that curves my perfectly painted red lips.

One of the cam drones notices me. It whirrs closer, the glassy eye in the center of its hovering body flickering as it scans me. There's some algorithm that's noting that I'm no one. Literally. No record of this face anywhere except a few innocuous docs in my strategically placed digital paper trail. But when I take a step, and then another, letting the sea-silk slither over my skin, the cam droid follows me. A few more join in.

I don't mind ending up on these recorders. I know how the drones work; my face is already deleted off its data banks. I'm not naive enough to think a sexy gown and a shiny red smile are enough to splash my image across the tabbies, but it is nice to be appreciated, even if by nothing more than robotic story-chasers.

Ah, well. I turn my back to the drones and head toward the security to get in. A bright digital screen hovers over the scanners, welcoming guests and reminding us of the theme of the event: *History as Art*, the words written in overlay atop various images of carefully curated feed of Earth—a flowing river, waves crashing on the beach, historical footage of now-extinct glaciers. Every year, the gala picks a charity to benefit. Sol-Earth is the subject of tonight's fundraiser, and, knowing what I know, it's no surprise there's a heavy emphasis on water.

"Just a minute," one of the guards at the scanners says, pausing the queue as she examines something on her screen. Half a dozen people are ahead of me, none of whom I recognize, but all of whom are used to being important enough to not be delayed. But not important enough for the guest-of-honor entrance happening in an hour.

"There wasn't this level of security last year," a man complains.

"You know it's got to be because of Strom," his date replies, smirking. Strom Fetor, tech trillionaire, guest of honor at the gala. She's probably right, but I tell myself that the scanners and the guards are for me. It's nice to pretend to be important when you get all dressed up.

The Museum of Intergalactic History stands imperiously atop a small hill. Ramps with moving treads curve along both sides of the white stone steps, and most people lining up used them. That wouldn't have made for quite as dramatic an entrance, though, and I don't mind waiting now.

I want to relish this moment.

Usually, Rigel-Earth is just a pain in the ass. The paperwork alone to get to this planet makes it absolutely not worth it. It's rare that I have stacked and coded invites and visas and a waiting docking bay, much less a pretty dress that lets me fit in with the richy-rich locals.

Here's the thing. We're all *technically* from Earth. I mean, real Earth. Sol-Earth. The original. But then we found other planets that could host life, and we named them Earth, too, distinguishing them by which sun they orbited. Centauri-Earth was first, of course. We all know the history.

Anyway, most everyone on Rigel-Earth is a dick. It's nothing personal, obviously; it's just statistically true. Rigel-Earth was super easy to set up compared to, say, Gliese-Earth, and it was discovered and ported really quickly thanks to some wealthy jerks who then leveraged their funding to ensure they and their buddies got first dibs on the best spots. They purposefully city-planned for their benefit, creating this hierarchy of towns that price out any of the workers who have to take the (admittedly kind of nice) public transport to work in the cities they've inflated to match their egos.

Basically, Rigel-Earth is the homeowners' association of the universe, and everyone knows it. The difference is, the people of Rigel-Earth think turning a planet into a gated community is swell, and everyone else thinks it's shitty. Who can be *proud* of being from a planet known to rig its own taxes and ensure only the elite can claim full citizenship?

Still, I let myself forget all my gripes as I perch atop the landing in front of the Museum of Intergalactic History. And I'll be damned if I don't pose a little in my shiny dress.

After all, at least some of these camera drones have to be linked to security feeds. If Rian's watching, I'm going to use the cool blue light to capture my best features.

I was lucky that I took the deal from my client at a station with a high-end tailor and charged my contact's accounts for the gown. This dress has crossed worlds to get to me—the raw material came from a seaweed in the oceans of Centauri-Earth. The blue-green base of the dress shifts in the light; the circle lums hovering nearby make the dress shine like a supernova. And tiny chips of glittering gems from Gliese-Earth litter the bottom, making rainbows scatter on the pale stone with every step I take.

There are tricks to clothing. The same effect could have been made with bits of glass sewn into the material or electric strands of illumination beads. But this place, these people? They would know the difference between real sea-silk and gems and knockoffs. Hell, even the cam drones would know the difference.

They're already buzzing off toward the hover ramps, bored with me. Someone whose face dinged a little check box next to *Important* must have showed up.

My eyes drift past the flurry of lights and drones and general static of anticipation toward the street below.

The MIH is in the most elite part of the most elite city

on Rigel-Earth. Built into a hill, a river wraps around the back end of the enormous building. In front, the street is carefully regulated—only someone with a scan pass can get any vehicle within spitting distance of the museum.

I knew this already. I know every entrance and exit into this building, from the receiving door for deliveries to the employee entrance in the back to emergency exits linked to alarms. As well as other possibilities—the grand corridor that cuts through the center of the building is topped with a glass roof, so if one were to need to get a little creative, well.

Anything can be a door with the right motivation.

It's not in the plan, but. You know. Just in case. Always nice to have options.

The line to get in still hasn't moved, and there's now a handful people behind me. My eyes skim past the gowns and suits to the uniforms. While the guests are loud, the guards are not. There's an undercurrent of tension. One looks up and happens to catch my eye. My gaze flitters away, suddenly enraptured by the dangling gem-crusted foot of Orion above me.

Thing is, this is a high-profile event. This is going to attract a lot of attention from a lot of people who like to cause trouble. And I would very much like them to just be chill tonight so that *I* can be the cause of trouble.

But there's a small crowd gathering in the park across the street. At least three dozen people, all wearing a white drape with a big red stamp on the shoulder. I squint, watching them, but I can't read whatever badge they're all wearing.

Great. A protest.

"Next," a guard calls, and the line moves forward.

The crowd gathering across the street all stop in a line parallel to it, heads tilted toward the museum. I can almost make out the circular red design on the drapes the people wear, but then they all lift their arms at once, raising their palms toward the sky.

Small glittering orbs rise up, hovering in a line above the crowd before zipping into patterns.

Oh, fuck me, Rigel-Earth even has pretentious protestors.

I wave a couple to go in front of me to the scanners. I don't have fancy holo specs on my eyes, but I know exactly what this is—a silent protest. About the charitable gala, no doubt. Anyone rich enough for an invite to this function would have specs, but I have to lift my wrist and hold my data band in front of my face in order to peep through it and see what the holo drones spell out in the sky above. My small purse dangles in front of me, attached by a magnetic clip to the band.

Squinting through the thin film on my data band, I see . . . a planet. Earth. My Earth, I mean. Sol-Earth. The holo drones aren't that great—only two contrasting colors, making it a bit hard to make out the details. But I guess not much detail is needed when the holo projection of my homeworld melts, lava-like slime dripping over the sphere until it's nothing. The drones swirl around, then spell out the message the protesters want the gala's attendees to see:

Let Sol-Earth Die.

Cam drones zip across the street, capturing the display for tabbies. Everyone tuning in across the galaxy is getting this message.

"Classy," I mutter, turning on my silvered heel and walking through the scanners. The guard waves me through. The only things in my wristlet are a small data recorder and lip gloss, nothing unusual.

Before I get through the main doors, I overhear one of the security guards talking into his cuff, confirming that the protestors have a permit and there's nothing they can do. The red badges. They're permits, bought and paid for, because nothing says activism like perfectly filed paperwork.

"They've only got an hour; just leave it," the guard says before looking up at me. "It's not like they're Jarra."

Even my blood runs cold at the name of that group. The Jarra are "freedom fighters" who want to rid Sol-Earth of every non-native by any means necessary and consider anyone who immigrated to one of the other planets to be a blood traitor. They want to separate Earth from every other world, cutting my planet away from the rest of the galaxy, and they have no qualms about being extremely liberal with the concept of "cutting." They're such a nasty lot, I don't ever take jobs with them, no matter what they offer.

Every job a Jarra does ends with blood.

I guess permits and holo drones are a little better than that.

The security guard's attention has shifted from his comms to me. I give him my best smile.

"Scan pass?" he says.

I hold out my data band. A moment later, his handheld reader flashes green. "Welcome to the gala, Ms. Lamarr." The guard holds his arm out, gesturing to the enormously oversized double doors flung open.

I take a step. Pause.

"What do they want?" I ask, casting a look over my shoulder at the silent protestors. Without looking through the film on my band, I can no longer see what the holo drones are displaying, just the glittering little orbs bouncing around the sky. The protestors below stare straight ahead. It feels like they're watching me, but there's a hollowness to their collective gaze that's deeply creepy.

It's part of the demonstration, I know that. Protests on Earth are messy, sometimes violent things. But protests on Rigel-Earth are scheduled and performed.

I would mock it, but . . . it *is* kind of getting to me. Unnerving.

"Oh, it's the aid tax." The guard waves his hand at them, as if he could brush the holo drones from the air.

"Of course," I say, smiling as I step past him and toward the entry.

The aid tax.

The aid for Earth. It makes sense to protest it here, at a charitable gala being held to raise additional funds for Sol-Earth's conservation.

But damn. That's gutting. Of all the taxes on this planet, of all the stupid elitist surcharges, the one that made three dozen people file a permit to send enormously expensive holo drones into the sky is the tax providing humanitarian relief to my home.

Fucking Rigel-Earth.

3

'm three steps into the museum when a firm hand grabs my elbow. I whip around and there he is, eyes and all.

"I knew you'd be here." He speaks in a low voice, biting off each word. There's no triumph in his announcement, only grim bitterness.

Well, that just won't do.

"Hello, Rian, how are you?" I make no move to pull my arm away from his grip; in fact, I spin a little closer to him. Flustered, he drops my elbow. But he doesn't step back. And neither do I.

I've seen him in a spacesuit, but I've never seen him dressed to the nines like this, all buttoned up and neat. It suits him. Very well. His white shirt has just two tiny triangles downturned at the collar over a silver ascot tucked into a vest hidden beneath a slick black jacket. A single white rose decorated with a black ring at the base is pinned to his lapel. I wonder if he got it from his family's luxury farms that sell produce for a premium. Roses are common on Sol-Earth, and it's hard to import flowers . . .

My mind wandered enough for this to get awkward. Then again, while I was staring at Rian's flower, he was taking in my gown, and the look on his face makes me glad I insisted the tailor cut slits in the material right at my hips, showing just enough skin to not be indecent while still inspiring indecent thoughts. Inspiring indecency is something of a specialty of mine.

"Isn't it ridiculous," I say casually, "how formal wear for men means layers and layers of cloth, but formal wear for women is the exact opposite?" I look down at my own chest, the neckline purposefully draped loosely so that, despite the secure design, it looks as if I'm one good sneeze away from scandal.

"What are you doing here?" Rian demands. Voice low. Warm breath, right on my skin. A laser-focus gaze that refuses to drop below my chin again, despite my best efforts.

"Invited guest." I flash my data band just to prove the point, my reticule swinging. He grabs my left wrist, inspecting the scan code. I lift my right hand, trailing my fingers along his knuckles until he looks up at me. "If you manhandle me one more time without my consent, I am going to hurt you," I promise sweetly.

He drops my arm.

But he doesn't step back.

And neither do I.

"I thought you may come, but . . ." he starts.

I bite my lip, watch as he watches. "You didn't think I'd come as a guest."

"Invitations are linked and tracked," he says, shaking his head. "I saw your name, of course . . ."

"Like my dress?" I do a little spin. "I got sea-silk just for tonight."

Rian's eyes crinkle. The clues are subtle but there— water imagery in the entry display, the color blue being used. Tonight's guest of honor and closing ceremonies being led by Strom Fetor, who owns Fetor Tech. All signs point to a certain announcement about nanobots being released into Sol-Earth's water cycle happening tonight. But he doesn't say anything. Doesn't want to give me a single inch, even if I already stole the mile.

I'm standing right in front of him, but he's looking for the con, not seeing me. And that just won't do. His eyes flick to the scanners at the entry.

"If you want to know what's in my purse, just ask." I pull on the strings, showing him inside. "What trouble could I get in with nothing more than a data recorder and some lip gloss?"

He flinches, then he glowers at the way I laugh. "You and a data recorder? Dangerous."

"I don't need a data recorder to be dangerous." But a girl does like to be appreciated for her talents.

"Ada." Rian sighs, his breath of frustration enough to

almost move my shellacked hair, coiffed and studded with little glittering gems at each lacquered wave. "What are you doing here? Really?"

I slip a little closer, just a hairsbreadth. Close enough so that my eyes meet his, but everything past them blurs out of focus. "I came to steal something, *obviously.*"

Blink. He leans back. Not much. "I knew you would come." He sounds disappointed. Odd.

I snort. "Well, that's a surprise to me. Because I was offered this gig months ago. I kept declining."

"Don't tell me you were considering giving up your life of crime."

"No, of course not." I laugh. "They weren't paying me enough."

"Who?" Rian latches onto that word. "*Who* wasn't paying you enough?"

"My client," I say, deflecting. "But that's beside the point. See, I only agreed to this job for one reason."

I let silence do the heavy lifting.

"And that is?" Rian asks when I don't elaborate.

I lean in close. Closer. The little hairs he's tucked behind his left ear sway with my word.

"You."

I wait just long enough to spot the goosebumps sprouting on his neck before I swirl away from him, the glittering hem of my gown brushing his legs. I tilt toward a group of people who've just cleared security and entered the museum. I can feel Rian's eyes on me, on the dress swishing over my curves, on the sparkle of silver flashing under my hem.

But I don't look back.

Rian can't approach me again without drawing attention. See, the thing is, I *do* have a legitimate scan-code invitation, linked to my name and identifier and everything. It's entirely legit. Plus, I've done nothing wrong.

Yet.

It's the same reason he couldn't arrest me when I stole the nanobot prototype and the coding from the *Roundabout*. Scavenge rights exist for any shipwreck that's not declared off-limits by the government, and the government didn't declare the *Roundabout* because they didn't want to draw attention to it, so that meant I could *technically* loot whatever I wanted. Fortunately for me, technicalities matter to someone who believes in the law.

But Rian still follows me as I drift through the galleries, floating between different groups, never lingering too long over any one display. As I predicted, the joint fills up over the next hour, more and more people cluttering inside. The MIH annual charity gala is strictly limited. Last night, the honored (rich) guests had their own private showing of the charity auction. The only way to get into *that* showing was to be hand-selected by the notoriously strategic gala director, Jacques Winters.

Today, attendance is still restricted, but the tickets to get inside were bought with cash, not connections. The open gala is still a big-enough deal that the MIH has been accused of influencing politics by granting tickets to one candidate over another. More typically, the only life-or-death situation happening here involves the vitality of a fashion designer's career, especially because camera drones are allowed inside during the closing ceremony, something not permissible during the prestige night.

The charity gala is a place for the rich to gather in one spot, preen about for each other, end up in all the tabbies, toss some cash around to look like philanthropists, and then trot off to be rich elsewhere.

The exclusivity is what makes this event work. I gaze around the crowded rooms. There are enough big names here to be a little unnerving, even for me. Without cams on the inside, deals get made. Handshakes happen without witnesses; promises are whispered in shadows. It's not just wealth here; there's power, too. Deals can happen in a place like this, unspoken agreements with more than one type of auction taking place.

No wonder Rian's on edge.

I nervously twist my earring, a little silver stud, the only thing I'm wearing right now that's actually mine. I'll sell off this gown later, and I have no use for silver shoes. My entire outfit is just a costume, with everyone here seeing only what I want them to see: A rich person blending into a crowd of rich people. Only Rian knows my dress is a disguise, but at least he appreciates how well I wear it.

Tickets to get in the door cost more than my ship, but my client paid for all of that, as well as arranging who among the guest list they could bribe out of a spot. Or, I don't know, maybe they had some sympathizer who was willing to hand it over for the greater good. All I know is they needed me inside to secure the asset, so they got me inside. They also gave me some pretty good tips on recon that I hope pay off in more ways than one, but as of this moment, I'm on my own. I either get what I came for and then get paid, or I don't. And if I don't . . . well, that would be pretty shitty. I wouldn't get paid.

Plus, I spent *every fucking cent* of my payment already. On credit. From someone I *definitely* cannot stiff. So, I better get the loot I've come here for. And I sure as fuck hope that what I bought was worth it.

There's also the minor fact that maybe Earth will die like those protestors outside want, but I'm just not going to think about that. There's pressure, and then there's *pressure*, you know?

Instead of thinking about how my Earth will die, I think

about how Rigel-Earth's main star is going to collapse in on itself and burn up this entire planet. Sure, it'll take a few million years, but that blue star will eat itself into becoming a black hole long before my sun will. *That'll show 'em*, I think, gazing at the crowd that will absolutely not be alive by the time any of that happens.

My eye catches Rian's. There have to be a hundred people in this one gallery room, clustered around and pretending to appreciate a climate-controlled box displaying a page that was ripped from Abd al-Rahman al-Sufi's *Book of Fixed Stars,* but somehow, the only one I see is him.

Which is why I walk straight into a woman, hard enough to make the gold bangles on her wrist clink together. Before I can apologize, she turns a thousand-watt smile on me, and I recognize her as a feed star. If we'd been outside on the street, I bet she'd have a bodyguard who would have made sure I didn't even share a city block with her, and if I did happen to klutz my way into her personal bubble, I doubt she'd look at me like a friend. That's what a seven-figure ticket price to get in the door will do for a girl: it makes everyone on the other side of that door think that riff-raff like me are filtered out, and that everyone left on this side is a friend.

Which is going to work great for me.

"Sorry," I tell the feed star, nodding congenially. She's really quite short in person; that's surprising.

"Not a problem, darling," she says, and I suddenly understand what a "sparkling smile" actually means. I make a note to watch more of her feeds.

"I love your dress," I say, because it feels like I have to say *something*. "Eva Charming?"

She laughs. "Who?" She makes a show of looking down at her gown before giving me the name of her designer. I make all the appropriate praises despite having no clue about couture, and the feed star smiles some more before drifting away.

Ostensibly, the gala raises money for Sol-Earth conservation, because of course they have to look like they give a damn about charity, and most people don't mind "saving the homeworld" to tick that box, even if it's not really charity. Anything that costs this much is about the show, not the benefit. There's not just the ticket price; there's the gems and silks and people paid to do hair and makeup and film it all for the feeds and negotiate contracts with the tabbies and ensure they're spotted—and recorded—being with the right people before coming inside. And let's be real—the museum gets its cut, Rigel-Earth takes a piece, the workers have to be paid . . . but the rest. I guess Earth gets that.

Which is something, at least.

Too much for the protestors outside, obviously. But they only minded enough to file a permit for an hour.

They did cause some buzz, though. I overhear more

than one of the other attendees talking about it. And most of them agree.

Earth's not worth saving.

It is, however, worth *buying*.

All the showrooms on the ground floor of the museum strategically highlight different items for sale. It's subtle—I suppose others would call it "tasteful." The big, open rooms have holos, art, and other exhibits, but it all directs people to look at what's on display in the center. One item per room— a historical artifact, a rare piece of art, a significant archeological find.

Available.

For a price.

This is the cost of charity to help Earth. We have to buy our aid.

By merit of being here, at the gala, each item will likely fetch an ungodly sum of money. That's the point, after all. But each item is also worth more than any price that could be paid. The last verified brick of the Great Wall of China, most of which was destroyed in the Second Eurasian War. A panel cut from the Bayeux Tapestry, preserved in a climate-controlled case. Feathers from the now-extinct North American bluebird. Each with a digital number beside it.

The current high bid.

4

The main gallery hall branches into several smaller rooms, each with a different display and a different item to bid on. I drift around. I know Rian's watching me; I can feel his eyes tracking my steps, but every time the crowd thins, I move on to another display.

I have been hunted before; it wasn't like this.

When I was younger, before the volcanic eruption at Yellowstone, my parents and I lived at the park. The park itself—by then privately owned, of course—was enough of a money-maker that some of the best security wrapped around it. I joke about how most civilized areas of Earth are under bubbles, but for the most part, that's not literal. Obviously, the bigger cities have protection, but there are plenty of smaller areas, mostly manufacturing districts or production zones, that just rely on people using their own gear rather than filtration bubbles. If it's raining, get an acid-proof umbrella; if it's sunny, take a radiation supplement.

At Yellowstone, however, the protection zones were

very literal. I mean, the area itself was over three thousand square miles, so there wasn't, like, a huge glass bubble over the entire park. But the tourists who came to Yellowstone were usually of two groups. One type liked the adventure and danger of a wild nature reserve. Extreme sports enthusiasts want a challenge, regardless of the planet, and having to backpack for survival appeals to some weirdos. And Yellowstone remained remote enough—before it exploded in a supervolcano eruption—that it wasn't *as* polluted as some other areas. Acid burns were only a danger during particular rainy seasons, and while pollution is slowly killing the planet, it does make for a gorgeous sunset, you have to admit.

So, vast areas of Yellowstone were left open, and the tourists who paid extra for the luxury of danger signed a lot of waivers before they were allowed to start hiking . . . and even then, patrols and carefully hidden fences along the paths helped keep the more dangerous mutations of wildlife at bay.

Literal bubbles were around some of the bigger, more well-known sites, with landhoppers carrying tourists from the plaque where Old Faithful used to be to the different sulfuric pools and hot springs. The waterfalls were still there, and although the water was, by that point, absolutely not safe to drink prior to treatment, the falls were still pretty, even through the clear, round protective zones. The tourism board did a lot to make the bubbles as unobtrusive as possible, and it was only in certain light that you could notice them anyway.

The environmental protection zones we had around the full-time staff living areas weren't as slick as the public-facing ones, but they were pretty sturdy. Around the housing units, there was the highest security—that's where the fencing was most obvious. To leave it, you had to physically go through a secure door cut into the composite protection material. But the park liked to pretend to be open, so after that, there was another zone that had no physical walls, just a combination of electrified fields and scented pheromone posts that "encouraged" wildlife—mutated or not—from crossing over. It was generally pretty safe during the daylight.

But obviously, none of us wanted to go out during the daylight.

During a party one night, my friends all started daring each other to cross the zones. This was just before the seismic activity got worse and people started evacuating, so I was young enough to think nothing bad would actually happen but old enough to be the exact right level of stupid to risk it.

Getting through the first layer was hardest—there were guards whose job was to make sure dumb kids didn't do exactly what my friends were egging me on to do. But I've always been good at improvisation. I got through the door, then found the boundaries to the secondary zone, the more open area. I decided a full lap around the housing units would sufficiently prove my badass-ness as a preteen who had stuff to prove and no reason to prove it.

Back then, both my parents were alive, Yellowstone hadn't exploded, the continental United States were still united both literally and figuratively, and while there were things that weren't the best . . . that moment, running under the stars, it meant something. I remember pausing, my back to the housing units, just looking up without any barriers and realizing how safe I felt, even if I knew it wasn't safe, and how big the sky was, how big the Earth was, how small I was.

I don't know. I can't define it.

But it meant something.

Even now, I can close my eyes and feel that night. Anything felt possible. All that mattered was being there, knowing that I had done something none of my friends dared to do, that I was unconquerable.

And then I went back inside the safe bubble of my home, certain of its permanence, its safety.

"You're a ghost," Rian says when I circumvent a crowd gathered around something or other.

His words are enough to make me pause.

"I've gone over every report we have on you," he says, matching my pace. "Aside from that spot of vandalism when you were younger . . ."

"Clean record," I say.

"Sparkling." He frowns. Good. That was money well spent. "And you have *very* good friends."

"I do," I chirp, then pause. "What do you mean?"

"You're an obvious security threat. I tried to have your name removed from the guest list and your ticket revoked."

"Bought and paid for," I say.

He lifts a shoulder. It doesn't matter if I have a ticket. He *could* have me kicked out of an event like this, what with me being a self-confessed high-security risk.

But apparently, I have *friends* that kept that from happening. Friends who have, no doubt, also been bought and paid for.

I suppose I should thank my client for that.

Rian's frown deepens. I slide my finger over the center of his forehead, down between his brows. "You're going to give yourself a headache," I say gently.

"*You* are a headache."

"You love me."

"I'm going to arrest you. You're here to steal something—"

"As I've mentioned."

"—and I *will* catch you. And your record will no longer be spotless."

Until I pay to get it blanked out again.

Rian glowers at me as if he can guess my thoughts. He probably can; I don't mind if he sees this about me. I like to watch him twist. I like to be the one to make him annoyed.

Nothing I did during my time on the *Halifax* with him was illegal. The *Roundabout* was a salvage, so taking anything from it wasn't stealing. Nothing I've done here at the MIH, so far, has been, either. And much as he thinks he can pin something on me now, he's wrong.

Even when I'm standing right in front of him, he still doesn't see what I'm doing.

After that night I left the protective enclosures at Yellowstone, for shits and giggles and just because I wanted to, I hacked into the security sys and downloaded the feeds the drones outside recorded.

It's important to know: To me on that night, there had been nothing but triumph and stars.

But on the feeds?

Another story. A different reality.

The night vision cams used old tech—it was just the staff

living area, after all; the park wasn't spending bucks on our security. So, the image that fed back to me was eerily ghost-like, my body bouncing in happiness, oblivious to the pale shadow padding silently behind me, the green eyes glowing with unwavering focus on my unprotected flesh. Timing was the only thing that saved me. I slipped back into the physical border just as the cougar crouched to leap at me, and even after the door was closed and locked, she prowled, tail lashing side to side, fury at her missed meal evident.

I had paused to gaze at the night sky and then trotted around outside without once even knowing that a beast was trailing me. I had felt so powerful, looking at the stars, but when I saw the cougar on the feed, I tasted ashy mortality on my tongue. My muscles, slim as they were, trembled.

I had not known I was being hunted.

And just because luck had drawn me to safety before the claws eviscerated my flesh made me no less prey.

I had felt victorious—that was the emotion threaded through my panting breaths and bright eyes. Triumphant joy. But it was only ignorance that had given me that false pretense, and every twinkling star in the black void reminds me of that moment, of how my insignificance does not extend to the possibility of my being a meal.

I turn now in the luxuriously appointed, hallowed halls of the Museum of Intergalactic History, my movement languid, sea silk swishing over my hips, glittering in the bright light of a planet lightyears from the shattered remains of the last place I felt safe.

Rian leans against the wall, waiting for me to make a move, watching, watching.

He thinks he's stalking me as I clack my silver heels from display to display. He thinks his law is as powerful as fangs and claws. He thinks I don't know an escape route, that I will have nowhere to run when he springs his trap, whatever that may be.

I have been hunted before. The difference is: I never felt the eyes on me, not like I feel Rian's eyes burning through my silk, searing into my skin. But there's a beautiful synchronicity to that, no?

His eyes never leave me, but all that does is confirm that even if he thinks he's hunting me, he's wrong.

I'm the predator here.

And he has no idea what I see.

5

I linger in the Egyptian antiquities room. The display is structured so that permanent museum items and information about the ancient empire are along the wall, with the auction item in the center—a canopic shrine and chest made for Pharaoh Tutankhamun more than a thousand years before the Common Era.

"I'm not going to steal it," I tell Rian. He's a few paces behind me, but when I speak, he gets closer. Good. I like him close to me. I like the way it makes my heart jump.

"I don't suppose it would fit in your purse."

I swing my reticule around as I take a step closer to the center display. As I watch, the number beside the canopic chest shoots up. I subtly look around, but it's impossible to know who's added to the bid. It might not even be anyone in the room. The people today are here to see and be seen. They may make token bids on some items—a random jewel from a random crown from a country no longer a sovereign nation, perhaps, or a piece of art from someone long dead—but the *really* valuable items have already been previewed by the *really* rich people, all of whom had an early showing of the displays away from the commoners who had to pay for the luxury of attending a charitable fundraiser.

Remote bidding.

"You do realize that this is a charity event," Rian says, but I'm not sure if it's to make conversation or if my face has betrayed my disgust. "To help *your* homeworld." Ah. The face, then.

I glance around the room. A few people I recognize—a Gliese-Earth politician, a singer, another feed star. There are more, some vaguely familiar, but I can't pin a name to any of them. Still, there's a chance I'm the only person in this gallery who was born on the same planet as Tutankhamun.

And there's a chance I'm the last person from Earth who will ever see this shrine.

"Can you imagine?" I ask Rian.

We could be anyone; we're just two people in a museum.

"Imagine what?"

"This man was born three thousand years before any human ever left Earth's gravity, and now his organs are on an entirely different planet."

Rian's eyes skim over the gilded shrine, the alabaster chest. The chest is carved with four openings at the top, one each for Tutankhamun's lungs, liver, intestines, and stomach. The number beside the chest blinks out, then goes up as a new high bid is placed. I could sell my own organs and still not be able to afford his.

"Ada, I—" he starts, but when I turn to him, his lips press closed. He watches me a moment, and I want to ask. I want to know. *What do you see?*

But it's not fun if he just tells me.

Rian turns back to the canopic shrine.

"No, it wouldn't fit in my purse," I say. The gilded wooden box is almost as tall as he is, and combined with the alabaster chest, I doubt I could even pick it up. "If I was going to steal this, it would require some planning."

I gaze about the room, noting the angles and positioning of the display, the way the cam drones hover nearby, the crowd. I bet the recessed edges at the doorframe hide a lock-down gate triggered if someone does so much as nudge the heavy chest.

I shake my head. "No, I don't think I could steal this from here."

Rian's eyes go wide. "Ada Lamarr, giving up?"

I snort. "No, not at all. If I wanted this? I would take it."

"But you just said—"

"Not from here. I'd talk *you* into buying it, and then I'd steal it from you." It's the best plan. If you can't take an object from one location, you just have to get the object moved somewhere else and *then* take it.

"Maybe I have better security than the museum."

I laugh. "Is this a theory you want to test?"

Rian moves closer to inspect the current high bid. A weird noise croaks out of his throat. "Well, it's moot anyway. My blood's not rich enough for this auction."

I shrug. "Then I just have to talk someone rich into buying it and then steal it from them." There are, after all, plenty of people mingling in the crowd who are the exact combination of rich and idiotic for a plan like that to work. Although, to be fair, *rich* and *idiotic* is a shockingly common combination in people. Inherited wealth is a hell of a stupefier.

Rian huffs a little laugh. Nearby, two people point out the carvings on the chest, the goddesses etched in stone and gilded wood, arms upraised. I'm reminded of the gala's motto.

History as art.

There's art here, yes. Undeniable.

I swallow hard, my throat dry. Just because art exists, should it be seen? I can almost hear a reply, a voice in my mind with a Rigel-Earth accent: *Of course. Art exists to be experienced.* And I don't approve of gatekeeping. For all my goals today, I actually quite like museums.

But not all art is for all people. And this art? It was meant for the dead. I inhale, exhale.

"You're angry," Rian says softly, watching me.

My heart leaps in response, further proof that I should not appreciate the art in front of me, the art not made for warm blood, attached organs.

"Furious." My tone is light, my rage as soft as breath.

He doesn't ask why, but I know the question sits on his tongue. Rather than give him a direct answer, I go to the wall, away from the canopic shrine and chest. "Did you know," I say, pointing to the display, "that people in Victorian England had unwrapping parties?"

"Unwrapping?" Rian starts, and then he sees the little informative graphic on the wall, showing an illustration of white men in stiff collars and women in swaths of taffeta standing around a table upon which lies a mummy.

"Some of them would eat pieces of the corpse," I continue. "They thought it was medicinal."

Rian's expression goes slack, but it's not enough. Because even in the image on display, the people dressed in gowns and tuxedos are portrayed as civilized. After all, the cutlery is placed precisely, napkins arranged just so.

"And then later," I add, "they ground the bodies up and mixed the powder with oil." I snort without humor. "Expensive paint, that. Mummy brown."

A little holo displays those words again—*History as Art*—overtop a series of paintings that used the pigment. A Delacroix melts into a Burne-Jones. They're taking that motto quite literally.

"At least—" Rian starts.

"Which is better, do you think? Medicinal cannibalism or corpse paint?"

Across the room, voices murmur in appreciation as the bid for Pharaoh Tutankhamun's canopic shrine and chest climbs higher.

"Or," I say softly, like it's an afterthought, "maybe the better question is, which is worse? The constant display of your sacred tomb in a museum, or a bidding war for your dehydrated organs?" I turn to Rian. "You see how this isn't better, right?" And for the first time tonight, there's doubt in my voice. Worry.

Rian shakes his head, and relief floods through me at the disgust evident in his features. "When does a person become an object?" he mutters, meeting my eyes with a clear, steady gaze.

"Historically, when someone else assigns a monetary value to them," I answer.

He nods, jaw tight, and whatever he sees on my face seems to satisfy him. He starts walking, sticking to the perimeter of the room. He doesn't feel like he can leave me, but he doesn't want to stay here.

He may be from Rigel-Earth, and his family may make their wealth through luxury food, but at least he knows enough to peel back the gold veneer of this party and see it for what it is. I wonder if this means he's crossed off Tutankhamun's crusty liver as a potential item for me to steal, or if my lingering attention sent the alabaster chest to the top of his list.

I watch him, the only art in the room that's mine to view.

And that's when I notice him fidgeting with his corsage. A white rose held down with a circular pin . . .

How did I not see it before?

A rose. A circle.

The *Rose*. The O-ring.

His pin is the exact same size and type of O-ring that I told him about when I was climbing out of a ravine lined with lava, the exact same O-ring that broke on the *Rose*, a ghost ship I discovered with a whole family dead inside.

Is this supposed to be some mockery of that moment? No, Rian wouldn't do that. Fuck, what's my evidence for that, though? *He didn't like mummy brown,* I think desperately, trying to hold on to the threads tying us together. But he's wearing that for me; he has to be. And the message is clear: he's going to find the O-ring in my plan, the flaw that will lead to my demise. *That's what it is,* I think, almost relieved. This is taunting me, nothing more, but . . .

He wears it as a badge of honor, just like the Victorians laying out a banquet.

I close my eyes and peel away the emotions I don't want to show, a different sort of unwrapping, a bitterer consumption.

When he finally looks back at me, I'm certain my face shows nothing. But just in case, I pull him closer to the shrine. "See there?" I say, pointing to the stone relief of a woman, her arms outstretched, her body facing the shrine, her back to us. There's one on each side of the box, each a different goddess.

"People think the Ancient Egyptians were showy, and maybe they were," I say. "But the goddesses face the box, not us." They know what they should look at, what they should not.

"It's for protection," Rian says. He nods toward the information scrolling above the display. "The four goddesses are both on the shrine and the chest, each providing a different layer of protection."

Layers of protection, each more elaborate than the next. It reminds me of bubbles at Yellowstone.

It reminds me of the cougar.

Of the volcano.

I glance at the O-ring on Rian's rose.

It reminds me that nowhere is safe.

Not even when you're dead.

6

Right, time to focus. Enough philosophical bullshit. I have a reason to be here. One goal. Well, maybe more than one. But Rian doesn't know that. And neither does my client.

I take a deep breath. It's just two cons, really. Do one job for my client, do one for me. And mine's a long job. I'm just planting a few seeds I hope to harvest later; that's all. No pressure.

I don't want to call *too* much attention to myself. I wander into the grand corridor, and Rian drops back, resuming his shadow role. Even if I can feel him watching me like a hawk, no one else throws me a second glance. I'm just another pretty dress in a room of silk. And I'd like to keep it that way.

The central hall is the museum's showstopper. The wide, open space is littered with cushy, backless seats covered in lush black-and-burgundy material that gives the appearance of burnt marshmallows. Above, cut-crystal panes cast prism rainbows over the white stone floor, the rainbows lost amid the elaborate costumes of the mingling guests. Whole feeds are dedicated to the fashion on display now, and I've got the insider scoop. There are the classic gowns, like mine, pretty dresses whose only purpose is to sparkle.

I prefer the bolder designs—the man painted in what looks like liquid silver, so shiny his chest could be a mirror, but with matte-black lines cut at odd angles so no one quite knows where to look at him. The woman whose gown is studded with mini holo displays, showing off constantly blooming flowers that open and close their petals with each step. My favorite is the man whose skirt billows when he walks, smoke and glittering sparks faintly visible under the dark material, like a storm cloud barely contained.

All the waitstaff are dressed in matching suits made of blue, watery-like material. I make a beeline to the closest one.

"May I offer you—" the server says, holding out a silver platter with twenty or so small plates of various delicious-looking concoctions.

"Yes, thank you," I say. I use both hands to take the entire platter, ignoring the rude way the staff member blinks at me, and head to an empty seat. The burnt marshmallows may be ugly, but they're at least big. I put the large platter down and sit beside it, plucking a plate off as I cross my ankles and gaze about the room.

The Museum of Intergalactic History is really big on

appearing authentic, which means it ironically looks like the old classical museums on Earth, emulating Ancient Greek architecture that was first translated through centuries and other countries and has now been strained through millennia and other worlds. But smooth, white stone blocks don't hide the security scanners perched atop the columns, and the silver-and-gold decorations do little to distract from the drone monitors hovering like bees above the crowd.

"You did a good job," I say.

Rian steps out from behind the column he was ostensibly leaning against, not quite out of sight but emulating stealth in the same way the museum makes a caricature of Greek academia.

"The security measures," I offer him graciously. "No one would dare steal anything here."

Rian doesn't try to hide his snort of disbelief. "I somehow don't trust you."

"No, seriously. I can't find a single flaw."

Emotion flickers over his face. He wants to be proud.

But he doubts me.

Cute.

He deflects by reaching for one of the small plates on my platter. I smack his hand away. "Get your own. I'm only here for the food, you know."

Rian snorts. "No, you're not."

My mouth is too full of some sort of delicate pastry for

me to quip anything back. I close my eyes, savoring the way the buttery, flaky crust melts on my tongue. I could fail this mission, and it would be worth my time for this moment. Not that I'm going to fail. But still. My contact should have opened with the free hors d'oeuvres; I would have taken this job faster.

I feel the seat cushion dip, and my eyes fly open, my hands moving to the plate on my lap so nothing spills as Rian settles in beside me. He's trying to be formal; he's sitting so that his back is to my right side, as if we're strangers.

Well, that just won't do. I lean against him, my head dropping on his shoulder.

"What are you here for, Ada?" he asks in a quiet voice meant only for me. "What are you trying to steal or sabotage or terrorize? Other than me."

"Don't be boring," I say gently. He has to know he's not going to get the drop on me.

He huffs a little laugh, the movement of his body rippling into mine. I let it happen, I let the momentum pass into me, I let the reverberations of his amusement vibrate through my bones. *An object in motion stays in motion.* That's what Newton said.

And that makes me think of the *Halifax*, where I met Rian. And First, Nandina, Saraswati, Magnusson. And Captain Ursula, my best friend, of course. They're still going. They'll keep going, too, job after legit job.

Not Rian and me.

Not us.

I use my finger to mash up the remnant crumbs on the plate and bring them to my lips, then swap the empty plate for one with a single jiaozi garnished with pickled ginger. When I bite in to it, the filling is . . . odd. It squeaks against my teeth, and I have to bite down harder than I should for a regular dumpling, even one that's been fried. My eyes track everything that remains on the platter.

"It's all supposed to be Earth food," I grumble. This is a charitable gala to benefit Earth conservation; this is supposed to be authentic. But just like the museum is a replica of a building in a nation that never existed on this planet, the caterers have used Earth recipes with Rigel-Earth ingredients. The jiaozi filling isn't chicken or pork. It's probably praxal, a meat far more readily available on this planet. I don't know if it's because the museum coordinator didn't think there was a difference or if they assumed their substitution was better than the original. Probably the latter. Typical.

"You've gone into each of the auction rooms," Rian says, and it almost sounds like he's reviewing notes with a subordinate.

I pick a cup this time, a little porcelain thing with gray mousse inside, a tiny silver spoon sticking out of the thick, sweet cream on top. Coffee-flavored with something sharper, some type of liquor. I've avoided the glasses of sparkling wine some of the servers offer, but this isn't much. Not enough to impair me.

Rian starts listing out some of the items in the auction, pausing, eyeing me. Waiting for a reaction. I eat through four more small plates. Wish I had more of that gray stuff. Delicious. Or something with peaches. That would have been nice.

Too soon, the food's gone.

"Have you heard anything I've said?" Rian asks.

"No." I clap my hands on my knees as I stand, making the gems on my hem tinkle like bells. "I told you not to be boring."

I take one step away, but Rian grabs my wrist, his fingers on the delicate bones under my palm, gently pressing into my pulse. His touch lingers, and my breath catches. I turn slowly, my eyes tracking his hand, up his arm, to his face, his eyes, their razor edge zeroed in on me.

I tug my hand, but rather than let me go, Rian stands, close enough for me to feel the warmth of his body even after he releases my wrist.

"What are you here for?" he asks.

"You," I breathe, unable to stop myself.

His eyes widen slightly. I've said it twice now, and he almost believes me, I can tell.

Almost.

I toss him my best charming smile. "Seriously. Come with me right now. We'll get on *Glory* and away from all these pretentious assholes and slip into a portal where no one can reach us." I lean forward, enough to make the people near us titter, intrigued, watching us through lowered eyelashes.

Rian's lips twist in disappointment, but his eyes sparkle. He loves the game as much as I do.

He just doesn't know he's the one being played.

I slip my arm through his, tucking his elbow in tightly. "All right, come with me," I tell him, striding across the hall.

There. The woman in red, the man by the door, the waitstaff member with a tray of empty glasses. They each glance at Rian, at me, away. They're with him, his organization. My contact's words clatter through my mind as I toss the woman in red a wink. *Rian White is a high-up on intergalactic relations. He's been tasked with the gala's security, but he will not be working alone.*

I dip past another member of the waitstaff, nabbing an extra dumpling right off the plate and stuffing it into my mouth before he even notices. I knew there would be more people with Rian here. It's not just because of me—the gala is a huge function full of highly important people including, unfortunately, tonight's guest of honor who'll close the ceremonies. The man by the door may be a bodyguard for an attendee, not with Rian at all. I can't be sure. I don't know the roster.

But I'd be a fool to ignore the fact that I can trust no one here. Everyone in this entire gala is either a mark or a badge. At least, that's how I have to treat them.

"What are you doing?" Rian asks as I pull him through the crowd.

"Having mercy on you."

He chuckles, the sound low and rumbling, and allows me to guide him to the back of the museum.

A big black curtain blocks the huge floor-to-ceiling windows overlooking the river. I noticed that earlier, but this area is far enough away from the bidding that it's clear it's been earmarked for a different purpose. As we get closer, I feel Rian tense.

"So, where are we going?" he asks, his tone trying just a little too hard to be casual.

This is where the closing ceremonies will be.

The black curtain extends across the breadth of the hall, but through gaps in the material I catch glimpses of flurried activity. As I suspected, the closing ceremony is going to be a bit of a production. I expect nothing less from the host's reputation.

Rian clearly thinks that's my target, so I veer abruptly left, toward the stairs. Most people take lifts; while these steps are stone and intended for guests, they rarely see use.

They're out of the way and close to the staff offices, which are somewhere beyond that black curtain.

"You need to ask yourself one thing," I say, releasing Rian so I can focus on the smooth stone and my absolutely useless, traction-less high heels.

"And that is?"

"Do I know where I'm going because I'm a museum aficionado, or because I've studied the floor plans to this museum so much while casing the joint?" I pause and cast him a look. "If it's the latter, does that make you an accomplice to my crimes?"

"So, you're going to commit a crime now?"

"Why can't I just be here for the history?"

"You're the one who brought up your lurid life of crime."

"You're the one who attached the word *lurid*." I pause so abruptly that Rian has to catch himself to avoid crashing into me. Nothing about this stairwell makes logical sense. The steps are wide but shallow, forcing a slow, meandering pace. They curve when they don't need to; I suppose for the drama of it—at this exact spot, I can see neither the floor where we left nor the floor above. Although we can still hear the tinkling of wineglasses and boorish laughter above an undercurrent of polite chatter, we're basically alone.

I sit down, letting my legs drape over the steps, and motion for Rian to copy me. He takes his seat cautiously, no longer bothering to quiz me.

"Did you know," I say softly, "this is one of the few spots in the entire museum where there are no visible security cameras?"

From the twist in his lips, I can tell Rian knew. And guessed that I did as well. Of course, drones could buzz up here and interrupt this cozy moment, but they won't. Not right now.

"Not much to steal in the stairwell," Rian comments.

"I don't know about that," I say, making a point to rake my eyes over his body. He's right, though—this little hidden alcove in the steps hides us, but nothing else. All the auction items are below, along with most of the guests. And above us are the permanent displays in the museum. Priceless, of course, but also highly secured, even more so than the stuff below.

Rian opens his mouth—so impatient, this one. I press my finger to his lips, lingering a moment too long on the warmth of him, the feel of his breath. I lean in closer, dropping my hand to the cold stone step. "For just a moment," I say, my voice low, "let's pretend that I'm only here for you."

Emotion flickers over his face, too fast for me to pin down what he's really thinking. All he says is, "And I'm only here for you?"

"Aren't you, though?" I don't hide the wry twist of my lips.

"Maybe." His eyes remain razor-sharp, but there's a

gruffness to his voice, a raggedy edge I want to further unravel.

I know that he means he's here for me in order to stop
me from stealing whatever he thinks I'm going to steal, but
I let myself pretend he's here because of me for entirely different motives. And in that impossible moment, I close the
distance between us, pressing my lips to his. I scoot closer to
him, my hands grabbing the back of his head, fingers lacing
through his hair. He's tense, a solid block of shock as stiff as
the stone beneath us, but only for a second, only until his
arms go around my waist, pulling me practically into his
lap, his mouth claiming mine in a kiss that's not hungry.

It's starving.

7

Oh, excuse me!" The woman in red, right on time, according to the schedule my contact got me alongside the tickets into this shindig. Well, I didn't know it would be her specifically, but I was betting that it would be someone from Rian's team. I break away from Rian, whose skin is flushed, eyes glassy.

And then he sees the woman who interrupted us. She has radiant dark skin, the perfect complement to the bright dress, and she wears her hair in braids that have been done up into two big, black buns atop her head, woven through with strands of lights that shift yellow-orange-red, like tiny licks of flame.

She fits in with the elite, but she's not one of them.

She's one of his.

They're *so* subtle, it's adorable, but I absolutely notice the way Rian's shoulders straighten, the way the woman bites the inside of her cheeks. She turns on her heel, heading back downstairs despite the way she had been going up before she caught us.

"What's her name?" I ask in a low voice. The way the woman's heels stop clicking for a microsecond on the steps tells me she heard, despite my best efforts.

"Phoebe," Rian allows, sighing.

Phoebe did not come up these out-of-the-way stairs because she was following Rian—he doesn't need a tail. And she wasn't following me, either, because that's Rian's job. Rian's my babysitter; Phoebe is someone else's.

I suppose *technically* I could be wrong. It's a guess that the person Phoebe's keeping an eye on happens to be my personal target on my little side mission today. But I got Rian on these steps on purpose. Okay, so, testing the no-cams theory was an added perk of that purpose, and I'm almost upset that Phoebe interrupted us, but Rian's not the only one who checked the guest list. If there's someone at the gala who needs an assigned person from the intergalactic security team checking up on him, it'll be the person I'm pretty confident is upstairs right now. Not because he's a security threat. He's the opposite.

He's an ideal target for someone like me.

Rian may think he's spent the better part of this evening watching me scout locations, but I was just acting on the information I'd gathered weeks ago, the information that told me I had time to kill.

The fact that Phoebe left without going all the way up the steps says that she's leaving the task of fetching my target to Rian. Not that either of them know my sights are zeroed in on their guest of honor. I'm pretty sure my meandering around the gala has thrown Rian off at least a little.

This is the one part of my plan that relies on chance. No, that's a lie. A *lot* of this plan relies on chance, which is why I don't like it. But this was a big chunk, and Phoebe, bless her, just tipped me off.

There's a man at the top of the stairs who has no idea I'm going to ruin him.

I glance at Rian, who still looks a little dazed. I'm going to ruin him, too, but in an entirely different way.

"By the way, you're welcome," I say, standing up and using the handrail so I don't slip in these horrifically useless shoes.

"For what?" His face is still flushed. I can practically feel the heat radiating off him as he stands up too.

I tap my lips. "Color-sealed." None of my bright red is on his lips, despite our impromptu make-out session. A look of horror flashes over Rian's face as he touches his mouth. His shoulders sink in relief when his fingertips come away without any crimson.

"Well, that was fun," I say, turning to continue upstairs, "but I've got work to do."

"On the second floor?"

"Mm." I head up the last remaining steps. "You've spent all this time worried about what I came to steal." At the landing, I turn, pushing a finger against Rian's chest, stopping him, then I lean in close, right next to his ear. "But I'm not here for something. I'm here for *someone*."

I can see the question already forming on his lips, so I move my finger from his lapel—right beside that fucking rose—to his mouth, shushing him as I jerk my head toward the door visible around the corner. A swath of light cuts over the white stone, a triangle of false gold made by electric lights.

"I'll give you this one for free," I continue. "I'm going into that room, and I'm going to talk to the man I know is inside. And if you want to listen at the door, by all means." I sweep my arm graciously toward it.

Rian's a step behind me as I swish my gemstones around and head inside the gallery room. His footsteps are silent, and they stop altogether as he takes my offer, eavesdropping.

Listening to exactly what I want him to hear and not a single damn thing more.

I *knew* his curiosity would get the better of him.

Inside, I ignore the man who looks up curiously at me as I inspect the display.

This room is large, with a sloping floor to showcase the metal desks lined up. Archaic black screens with various dials, meters, and buttons are interspersed along the four rows of metal desks, each painted a pale bluish-greenish color a step above pastel. There are no chairs behind the desks, but I spot the black receptors to indicate an interactive display.

A thin red line surrounding the display warns people not to get too close to the artifacts. On the far wall, digital displays recreate a map of the land masses on Earth as they were centuries ago, as well as a series of numbers and letters and data that mean nothing to me.

And there, off to one side of the desks, exactly where I expected him, right on time: Strom Fetor.

My dress isn't exactly whisper-quiet, and the middle-aged white man homes his attention in on me, raking his eyes over my body. He wears the humored smile of someone used to being unthreatened and unbothered.

I hate him *so* much.

"Hello," he says. His sight is glued to me; Rian's stayed out in the corridor, so it looks like I'm alone. I should not like the way Rian follows my orders so precisely, but I certainly do.

"Hello," I say.

Strom Fetor doesn't know me from a hole in the ground, but that's fine. I know him. And he's exactly who I've been hoping to meet today. See, I knew Rian would be here.

Fetor? A bit of a gamble.

Not in terms of the gala, of course. Fetor was announced ages ago as the host, and he's going to be making the end-of-the-night speech. But I had to do my research to figure out when and where I could corner him alone. *Well,* I think, considering Rian outside, *mostly alone.*

My stomach twists, though I don't let any of that show on my face. See, I *really* like plans that are simple. Smash-and-grabs, that's my style. The *Roundabout* job? I wasn't even supposed to be seen, much less make my way into the *Halifax* crew. I work alone, and I prefer to be a shadow on the wall, easily overlooked. That's the only reason I'm wearing glittering jewels and shiny sea-silk tonight: at *this* gala, *this* flashy costume is what I need to blend in.

But I'm my own worst enemy.

My client's job—yeah, that's basically smash-and-grab-style, easy-peasy, I've already got it in the bag, even if Rian doesn't realize it yet.

But *my* job, this little side hustle? It's a long con. And while finding a way to take down Strom Fetor is a nice little side perk, it's about more than that.

And it's not going to be done any time soon.

It relies on multiple moving pieces, some careful manipulation, and a little bit of luck.

And tonight? Tonight, I'm just tipping over the first domino.

"Surprised to see anyone leave the ground floor," Fetor says.

"That's me." I smile, tightlipped. "Surprising."

"What's your name?" He doesn't offer his own name, because he knows I know it. *Everyone* knows Strom Fetor, whether they want to or not. To some, he's an innovator. He owns half a dozen companies, at least. Got his start in medicine before going into communication, buying himself the CEO position of the portal-comm tech that every ship in the galaxy uses to ping messages through the black. That set him up for a reputation of being a genius, at least to the people who just see his name plastered on their tech and think that means he's smart enough to have invented it.

"Ada Lamarr." I move farther into the room, putting the main display between us, nervously fidgeting with my earring as I studiously ignore Fetor. I read the info hovering above the massive multi-person metal desk while Strom Fetor tries to read me. But while I can tap my cuff band to make the language on the display shift to one I know, I'm indecipherable to him.

> Mission Operations Control Room 2: the Flight Control Room for Apollo 11, the first crewed Moon landing in human history.
>
> This room replicates the MOCR 2 used during the Apollo missions performed by the National Aeronautics and Space Administration, an independent agency of the United States of America on Sol-Earth. All artifacts on display are restored originals.

"These are the exact same units used in the twentieth century to put a man on the moon," Fetor says, which is the exact same information I just read. He steps past the tiny line of red light caging the desks.

"Aren't alarms going to go off?" I ask, raising an eyebrow.

Fetor smiles at me, and I want to puke, because I can tell he wanted me to ask him just that. "They turned off security in this room for me."

Of course they fucking did. No laser barriers, no security drones, just Phoebe coming to check up on him and remind him of the schedule. Strom Fetor could buy this whole museum. The rules do not apply to him.

Which means they don't apply to me, either.

Convenient.

I cross the security laser line too. No alarms go off. Handy little trick, that. All you have to do is be rich, and you can take anything.

Then again, I knew that already.

My hand trails the cool metallic surface of the desk. Above us, the display switches from informational text to a holo. Light shoots down from the ceiling, creating the images of chairs filled by people in front of each station of the recreated control room. The people—mostly white men— generally wear button-down shirts with collars that are far too wide and thick glasses. Muted sound pipes into the room, recreating chatter from ancient transcripts.

Fetor steps closer to me, his hand going to a red, boxy item on the table. As soon as my eyes land on it, it triggers a display drone that gives additional information.

Actual _telephone_ that provided a direct line between NASA and the United States of America's Department of Defense. Read more?

I do a hard blink, sending the data away, although I'm tempted to select the word _telephone_ and double-check the definition. I've seen phones before, obviously, but not one like this, so big and wired. Fetor lifts up the receiver with the coiled red plastic-coated wire and holds it so one round part is by his ear, the other by his mouth.

"Houston, we have a problem," he says, grinning at me.

I step back, putting some distance between us. His grin falters but just a tiny bit. I think about Rian outside. Apparently, I'm enough of a threat to stalk across the whole museum; Strom Fetor, meanwhile, can ignore security and play with centuries-old historical artifacts and that's just fine.

I lean my head back, letting the holo-projector lights pierce my vision. When I look up, he's watching me, a gleam in his eye like he has a secret. "Wow," I say, awe threaded through my voice like a glimmer of lightning in a storm cloud.

"Wow . . . what?" Fetor smiles, clearly thinking he's in on some joke as he puts the telephone receiver back down in the cradle.

Crooked.

That artifact was used during the original Space Race, a witness to the unbelievably high tension in the room as the entire world waited to find out if men could escape the bonds of Earth or if they would die in the attempt, and this asshat puts the receiver down crooked.

Ugh.

I cut my eyes to him. "Wow, I really, *really* hate you." I roll my shoulders back. It helps, actually, to be honest like that, even if I spoke in a friendly voice to counter the harshness of my words.

Fetor's eyes widen a little. "You hate me? You don't even know me."

See, that's why I fucking hate him. Of course I know him. He has more wealth than my entire homeworld. He's always on feeds and lives for the tabbies. And that's just the publicly available data.

What I *want* to do is shove him against the metal desk and punch his smug face in. But I don't. I can be civil. Well, mostly. When I'm paid to be.

Fetor decides to ignore what I said. I can almost see him consciously shrug off my very clear and explicit opinion of him. *Surely, she doesn't hate me,* I can practically read on his face, like a drone displaying data over his head. *Everyone loves me. She must have been joking.*

"I think I'm going to buy this," he says, shooting me a conspiratorial look. "It would be funny."

We have vastly different interpretations of *funny.*

"The telephone?" I ask. "For your communications office?"

"Oh, that's good," Fetor says, nodding appreciatively. "I was thinking of the desks, but the phone . . . yeah . . . ." He probably thought it'd be funny to put a mission control center in his house or something, which isn't funny at all. I, on the other hand, am actually quite hilarious, and I can see the moment he connects the facts and decides my idea was his all along.

"Exactly." He wags a finger at me. "You get it. The comm office should totally have this."

"Problem," I point out. "It's not in the auction."

Fetor shrugs. That's not a problem to him.

"Hello, Mr. Fetor," Rian says, announcing himself as he steps into the room. I guess he didn't think he'd hear anything important. That's what he gets for not paying better attention. If he'd waited just a little longer . . .

Fetor doesn't look surprised to see him. But his eyes do widen when I stride over and slip my arm through Rian's, pulling him close.

"You know each other?" Fetor asks.

"Not really," Rian says at the same time I say, "Absolutely."

Fetor's eyes switch to me, a wry look at my conflicting answer. I cup my mouth in a faux stage whisper and say, "Rian's *mine*." My fingers tighten in Rian's elbow.

"I don't get a say in that?" Rian asks.

"Nope." I don't let him go as I lead him farther into the room. "Fetor here is going to buy this historical exhibit to use in his communications office," I tell him.

Fetor beams like this is something to be proud of, as if his communication network was worthy of stealing—I mean *buying*—a display out of a museum.

I fucking *hate* him. I know I said it before, but it bears repeating. He's such a sham. Fetor himself did *nothing* to develop the tech needed to make portal comms work, just like he did nothing with his prior businesses. He just swooped in and bought the company after the tech was already in prototypes. Being the money behind a project is nowhere near the same as being the brains. Anyone can have money. Especially people like Fetor, who was born into it.

I mentally shake myself.

Can't get distracted now.

I turn to Rian, a much more appealing face to look at. I smile sweetly, full of innocence. "Was it Fetor's communication office that developed the new nanobots for Sol-Earth?"

The color drains from Rian's face.

Fetor, meanwhile, barks in delight. "Oh, you told her about that? Well, keep it secret for another hour or so, sweetheart." Bastard's already forgotten my name. "The official announcement is tonight, right, Rian?"

"Tonight," Rian chokes out. "And right now, you're supposed to go down now for a last tech check, Mr. Fetor."

That's what Phoebe was coming up to remind him about. That's what's behind the black curtain in the grand corridor—a hover stage and probably a pretty elaborate light show to go with it. That Fetor's style. And while cams aren't allowed in the charity gala, the closing remarks are recorded live and fed through all the tabbies.

"This is Strom Fetor," I tell Rian, waving my hand in the man's direction. "He invented most of the tech being used tonight. I don't think he needs a rehearsal."

I'm an amazing liar. Rian glares at me, but Fetor chuckles smugly. "We'll be fine. I've already gone over the specs. Well, my people have. Lighten up, White. It'll go off without a hitch!"

"Yeah, White, lighten up," I say, smiling at him. Rian looks like he would very much like to murder me, which makes my grin even bigger. "What a grand finale this is going to be."

That was a guess, but neither of the men object, so I figure I'm right. Fetor's speech is the conclusion of the gala.

And during that speech, he's going to announce a plan to "save" Earth with the climate cleaners.

His announcement is at the end of the night so as not to reduce any bids at the charity auction. Get everyone to donate for Earth's conservation before showcasing a possible solution that's already in the works.

Clever. I bet it was Rian's idea.

"Hey, did you see the protestors I hired?" Fetor continues, oblivious. "I tipped off some of the tab reporters to cover it in advance. Should make a nice, contrasting point to the story, no?"

Rian drags his eyes from me to Fetor. "You should have cleared that with security."

Fetor shrugs. "Think of the headlines. Early feeds are focused on the protests, not whatever designer made Luxa Ng's gown. Leads right into our announcement tonight." He spreads his hands out, envisioning the headline: "*Strom Fetor Leads Way to Cleaning up Sol-Earth's Broken Climate.* And then we can open with a quote about how generous of a donation I gave."

There it is. The reason he's doing this.

The credit.

Earth needs saving. And he'll do it.

As long as he gets the credit.

8

So, about this announcement," I say.

"Ada—" Rian starts.

"Hush. So, you're going to let everyone know about the climate cleaners tonight?"

Fetor nods. "We had a bit of a hiccup with them earlier." He punches Rian in the arm, and while it seemed to be a genial gesture, that punch had weight behind it. Dick. "Which is why the government enlisted the aid of the private sector."

The nanobot prototype and the coding for the climate cleaners were secured on the *Roundabout*, and it was absolutely not the government's fault that the ship crashed into a planet.

It was mine.

(Partially, anyway. Unlike some people in the room, I don't try to take credit for *everything*.)

"Did you know," Fetor continues, "that some anarchist group tried to steal the data? What kind of monsters would steal data that's meant to aid the billions of people on such a desolate planet?"

"What kind of monsters, indeed," I say, smiling at Rian innocently. "I bet they would do something horrible, like try to exploit the people of Earth, make them pay for their own survival."

"Which is why the government is funding the project," Rian interjects, glaring at me.

"Because you can *always* trust the government to handle large programs like a climate-cleaner system that will affect an entire world. If there's one thing we can say about the ol' UG, it's that it's efficient."

Fetor snorts, his eyes raking over my dress. "Oh, I like you."

"The feeling is very much not mutual," I say pleasantly. "So, anyway, you're going to buy this room?"

Rian's jaw is tight. He doesn't like that Fetor can—and will—buy a piece of history. But he can't protest. Yay, capitalism.

Fetor opens his mouth to speak, but I hold up my finger. My heart's racing. I love this part of a con. "But I thought," I say, the boiling anticipation within me making my words bubble out, "you would buy something from the Skye Martin display."

Rian glares at me. *Don't give the trillionaire ideas,* he says with those razor eyes.

I ignore him.

"What makes you think I want something from that room?" Fetor asks.

He doesn't, and I know he doesn't. Here it is, though. The tricky play. I don't need Fetor to go to the Skye Martin display, but I do need him to get out of here. Just long enough for me to make sure that domino falls in the right direction when I flick it.

I'm so excited I almost want to throw up, but I am not going to waste all that good food from earlier.

"I'll confess," I say, grinning sheepishly at Fetor, "I did a little reading up on you when I found out I was going to be attending the gala." It goes without saying that Fetor would be here; he attends every year, even when he's not the guest of honor, and every year, he makes a splashy show of wealth. Sometimes, he bids on an item in the auction, but only if there's something for his collection. The man has well-known affinities for certain items. "I scoped out the items downstairs."

"Nothing of note," Fetor allows.

Tell that to Tutankhamun.

"So I figured, where would a man like Strom Fetor be? Definitely in the early-space-exploration rooms."

Fetor does that weird thing with his mouth where he's trying to pretend he's not smiling but definitely wants people to see that he's pretending he's not smiling because he's just that damn modest. "My reputation proceeds me."

"Precedes," Rian says, barely audible, and now I'm the one biting back a smile.

"The Mission Control Room is pretty . . . classic," I say, finally settling on a word as if it was disappointing. "But have you seen the Skye Martin portal display?"

"Of course I have," Fetor says.

I toss him a shy smile, entirely fake. "I've never seen it before." Rian glares at me. I wonder if he scoured the security feeds enough to know I've visited it several times.

"You've never seen it?" Fetor gapes at me. "You know, you could come to visit my estate as a guest. I actually bought part of the portal a few years ago. It's in my garden."

"Or you could look at the display that's literally down the hall," Rian growls.

Oh, jealously is hot on him. And also, he *doesn't* know about my little scouting missions. Slipping there. Nice. I enjoy being his blind spot.

"I suppose that's quicker," Fetor says. "But the offer stands. Here, let me show you the display."

Fetor strides toward the door, Rian at his heels. It takes them a few moments to see I've not followed, but that's all the time I need.

Rian whips around, his eyes snagging on every detail of me standing by the metal desk, the red telephone receiver in my hand.

"Sorry, the way the receiver was crooked was scratching at my brain. I had to fix it." I settle the receiver down on the cradle correctly, the coiled red wire coming off it looped in a neat circle.

First domino: down. The rest will take time, but for now? I can let Newton's law work all by itself.

Fetor waits for me to catch up to him. I pass by Rian, whose narrowed gaze traces a path from the red telephone all the way to me. I loop my hand around Fetor's arm just to piss Rian off.

"I love the way communication evolves," I say as we head down the corridor. "That red telephone, it was a direct line to the Department of Defense. I suppose they needed it if the space shuttle blew up or something. And it was secure. One telephone at the NASA Mission Control, one telephone at the Department of Defense. That's real security. We don't have that anymore."

Fetor looks down at me. "We have security."

I give him a pitying look. "And yet some anarchist group stole your original nanobot prototype."

That makes him stop. Fetor looks from me to Rian, eyes wide, a pale pink flush on his pasty cheeks. "*My* company didn't break security," he says, a little too loudly. "*My* company protected the data with a private shipment and multiple stages of unbreakable technology."

Unbreakable. Okay.

"You really shouldn't be talking about this," Rian starts.

Fetor waves aside his concerns. "We're all friends here."

"Not me," I say. "I hate you. Remember?"

Fetor laughs in a tone I'm sure he thinks is charming. "Anyway, that security breach—not my fault. Whenever the government gets involved, you have to expect certain . . . flaws."

Rian looks like he wants to add something, but I know he's not going to confess that it was actually me who stole that data.

"Besides, it all worked out in the end," Fetor continues. He pats my hand, still in the crook of his arm. "And while there was a breach initially, the final nanobots are securely in the Sol-Earth communications tower. And *no one* can get inside that I don't personally approve of."

Which is why my client hired me to do just that. I mean, not *technically*, but hey. I've got agendas of my own.

I fake ignorance a little longer. "I just don't think anything is really secure in this day and age. Certainly not information." I cast a sidelong glance at Rian. "Just think: with enough time and a data recorder, any file could be stolen."

An adorable little muscle tics in Rian's jaw. I don't want him to have an aneurysm, but if he does, I do want it to be because of me.

"Not in my offices," Fetor says firmly.

My whole body melts with happy bliss. I love breaking confident men.

"Let's change the subject," Rian say even more firmly.

"To what?" I ask, my tone bright.

"To anything that doesn't require a high level of security clearance."

Fetor chuckles.

"So, you're announcing tonight that the climate cleaners are going to be released soon," I say. "I assume they'll be going out of this super secure office of yours?"

"That's on a need-to-know basis," Rian says, cutting Fetor off from telling me everything. Fine. I can work for my information. But also, he just confirmed what I asked, so that was nice of him.

"And here we are. The Skye Martin room," Fetor announces, sweeping his hand toward the gallery display.

The museum has a portion of an actual portal on display. It's been deactivated, obviously, and the power core's been taken out. It's only a fraction of the ring—with one part in Fetor's backyard, apparently—but even so, it's massive.

Fetor starts talking like he's a professor in a lecture hall, but I can easily block his voice from my mind as I move around the display. When will men realize that just because they speak doesn't mean anyone's listening?

Unlike the Mission Control Room, this display is designed to be interactive. I'm allowed to go right up to the portal ring and touch it. My hands trail over the metal edge. Here, the wall of the ring is as tall as my chest and wider than two Rians standing on top of each other. The curve goes all the way up to the ceiling, giving it the illusion of continuing through the plaster.

Fetor pauses in the endless drone of misinformation that I've long since tuned out, and I use that opportunity to activate the holo for the room. The lights project a woman in a thick space suit floating out of the ceiling like a ghost, her face obscured by a mirrored visor on her helmet. She's got a heavy, clunky LifePack on, and she doesn't have jaxon jets, which is a shame, because someone like Skye Martin deserved jaxon jets. She was just born before they were invented.

"There she is. The woman who invented portals," Fetor says, pointing to the holo projection.

Skye Martin didn't invent portal travel. She was born on Centauri-Earth, which means she wouldn't have even been on a planet other than Earth if portal travel hadn't already been invented. Portals are the only thing that allow faster-than-light travel.

What Skye Martin did was make it even quicker. She combined solar glass—a rare material that's only ever been found on a handful of worlds inhabited or not—with portal tech to make portals faster and more reliable. Without her, it would take months or years to go between worlds. Now? Weeks. Days for some paths.

When I look over, I see Rian watching me, as if he

thinks I could pick up this piece of a portal and hide it under my tight-fitting sea-silk dress.

"Mr. White, Mr. Fetor?" a voice says from the door.

We all look up to see Phoebe, Rian's associate in the red number, standing tentatively. She looks a little frazzled. Up and down the steps, wrangling wayward men. Not the best job to have.

"Hello, Phoebe," I say. She nods at me, but her attention is on Rian and Fetor. "Love your dress."

She glances at me as if she'd forgotten I was here. "Thanks," she says, her attention already drifting back to Rian. "It's an Eva Charming. Sir, we really need to complete the tech check with the addition of—"

"It's fine; it's just a tech check," Fetor says waving her off. "I *invented* the tech."

"And it's still in prototype," Phoebe says cooly. So, picking up on the way she doesn't let emotion inflect her voice, this fancy-hover stage thing with a fancier nanobot display isn't exactly ready for showtime.

"Also, the people operating the stage didn't invent it and have never worked on something like it before." Rian sighs. "I'll go with you and make sure it's quick."

"Have fun, bossman," I tell Rian with a mock two-finger salute.

Rian's eyes narrow. "Phoebe, did you ensure the security was back on in the Mission Control display?"

"Of course," she says, all efficiency. Rian pauses, saying something low to her, and her eyes zero in on me, narrowed, suspicious.

That's that, I guess. Rian's off to do more boring things, and he's set his watchdog on me instead.

Fetor turns to me as he heads out. "Lovely meeting you."

He still can't remember my name. "I regret every second I've spent in your presence, and I want to stomp your face in," I say genially.

"In those shoes?" Fetor makes a point of staring at my silver heels. "Some people would pay good money for that."

Well, now he has my attention. "Really?"

"No," Rian says forcefully. He grabs Fetor's arm, pulling him toward the door.

"Wait, no, let me hear him out. Good money?" I ask.

"Very good." Fetor's lecherous grin may be the only real emotion I've ever seen his plastic face wear, and it promises a price tag with a lot of zeroes, my favorite kind of number.

"*No,*" Rian says again, already in the corridor.

"Maybe later," I call to Fetor as Rian drags him away.

9

The woman in red watches Rian and Fetor go as she stands in the doorway. After enough time has passed that they're definitely down the stairs, she turns to me. Gone are the timidness and polite veneer. "The fuck are you doing?" she asks, stepping farther into the room.

"You're supposed to ask me the codeword," I point out.

Phoebe rolls her eyes. Technically, I am the only one who needed the "Eva Charming" link as a codeword so I could identify the contact on the inside if I needed to—apparently, the contact already knew who I was. Which makes sense now that I see my contact works *for* Rian. Bit unexpected, but I can roll with it.

There's an irony, too, in the fact that my contact on the inside was also assigned to Strom Fetor—although perhaps Fetor doesn't have a dedicated security team like I thought, and she was only fetching him for the tech trial. The pieces start organizing themselves into a pattern in my head: Rian was tailing me, Phoebe was watching us both, and she put herself in a position to get to me alone.

"If you're already in UG security, why does the client need me?" I ask.

"I don't have high-enough clearance to get in. Rian's the only one in our department with full access." Phoebe strolls languidly around the room, eyes tracing the enormous portal built inside.

I feel a little sorry for the portal. This thing is made with minerals mined on multiple worlds and had been filled with fuel generated from the captured sunlight of stars so distant that humans once only theorized they were there. It hung in space, defying the void, allowing intergalactic travel for nearly a century before it was replaced.

And now it's caged in a windowless room.

I give it a little pat, like it's a puppy. It deserves better.

I can feel her watching me. Phoebe. She's not telling me the whole story; that's for sure. Not that I blame her. I've got secrets of my own. But it's not just about clearance.

I'm betting she tried to be honest first. The good sort usually do, and she seems like Rian, all noble and sincere and hoping to do the right thing. So, I'd wager, when she first realized just how colossally Strom Fetor's company was going to fuck Earth over, she tried to raise the alarm internally. I'm betting she even approached Rian. But she didn't have the evidence, I suppose, to make him see how bad this deal was going to go.

I glance at her out of the corner of my eye. She's not like

me; she wouldn't have tried to turn her knowledge into profit. And I was wrong, I think; she didn't go to Rian. Because Rian would have listened to her. She went to someone else. Someone who doesn't care the way he does. Maybe someone higher up the chain? Yes, that'll be it. She tried to tell someone, and they didn't believe her.

So, she's done with words. Actions only. Except now she's burned some bridges that would have helped her do more from the inside. Lost a promotion, maybe, or an ear. Now she's stuck as a junior member of security, fetching assholes to do tech checks. She sacrificed something in an attempt to do the right thing, and it didn't pay off.

It usually doesn't.

I wonder how different things would have been if she'd been trusted when she spoke up.

But that's an old story, often repeated throughout history. It's rare that anyone listens to words they don't want to hear, rarer still when the speaker's not the one in power.

"Have you even started on the mission?" Phoebe asks, pulling my attention back to her.

See, well, that's an interesting question. The mission the client hired me to do? I mean, technically. But I'll confess, I did sort of get distracted by my secondary goal, knocking over dominoes just to see them fall.

That's what my contact gets for not paying for the repairs on *Glory*.

Still, I do have a real job to do. And I've done . . . some. I've laid some groundwork. That sounds good. "I've laid the groundwork," I tell Phoebe confidently.

She raises her eyebrow, all doubt. Obviously, she's been working with Rian for too long.

"What's your connection with Fetor?" she asks.

"None. Why do I have to keep reminding everyone how much I hate him?"

Phoebe frowns at me. "You're supposed to be here for—"

"I know," I say, cutting her off. "And the asset is all but secured."

More eyebrow gymnastics.

"Really," I say.

She sighs like she's five decades older than she really is. "Could you just stop with whatever games you're playing with Fetor?"

"You got it," I say.

She rolls her eyes, not believing me. "You've 'laid the groundwork,' eh? I'll have to hope that's enough. This entire project has been a mess. The whole thing. Took forever to get the planning in and the prototypes developed, and now that the climate cleaners have been approved, everything's a rush job."

Things get sloppy when they're rushed. Cracks start to show. Things fall apart.

Exactly the kind of chaos I thrive in.

Phoebe cuts me a glance. "And Fetor *insisted* we announce the nanobot program tonight. I can't even tell you the number of security breaches we've already stopped."

I knew this event would be a draw. Ugh, competition.

"Fetor likes the spotlight," I say.

Phoebe snarls in disgust, which makes me like her even more. "It's all a show to him." She describes a little of what's happening later—a hover stage that's going to soar out over the guests, with holo projectors doing a three-sixty wraparound display as the galaxy is informed of the Fetor Tech-funded climate cleaner innovation.

"Sounds big," I say. *Sounds easy to break,* I don't say.

She shakes her head. "Too big. We *finally* got the whole stage offline, so it's not attached to any network, but . . ." She shakes her head harder, braids dancing. "It's too fucking much."

So, Phoebe sees the flaws too.

I try to get a bead on the situation, on her. I knew my client had someone on the inside—a volunteer, a *believer.* Phoebe may have been recruited . . . but she doesn't have Rian's security clearance to get the job done. The government is wasting her, using her to put out all these little fires rather than giving her more access.

While I've been thinking, Phoebe's been watching me. "You're missing an earring," she says.

I touch my left ear. Observant. I shrug like it doesn't matter.

I could use a distraction, though. If she's in it for the charity instead of the money, I'm betting she's a local girl. Judging from her accent . . .

"American?" I guess.

"Like you."

I hate that she knows more about me than I know about her. *And* she's getting it from two sides—she's got what little information my client knows about me as well as whatever Rian's been able to root up. And while I paid quite a coin to make sure records on my background were purged . . . I don't like the situation. We'll just leave it at that.

It's easier to be a ghost. It's better to be gone before I'm even spotted in the first place.

And here I am, in a glittering gown for every eye to see.

Food's good, at least. Still, there's a difference between smiling for camera drones that will delete my unimportant face, and my actual name being read by people who know to link it to me.

"So, what's your angle?" Phoebe asks.

"Same as yours."

She snorts, the sound full of contempt and derision.

"We could not be more opposite," she states. "I'm not paid for helping."

"You are," I say. "Just not in cash. So, what part of America were you from?"

She hesitates but ultimately finds nothing too offensive about the question. "Indiana."

"Oh, not bad." Indiana was far enough away and east of the supervolcano when it erupted. Close enough to give her a healthy desire to actually give a shit about fixing up Earth's problems.

"Not great," she says. She was probably raised in a free colony—an area that didn't have the intergalactic-tourism draw to be developed, but enough farmland and stable ground to independently subsist as a community.

It's amazing how people just keep going. Supervolcanoes, climate collapse, global pandemics, dissolution of society . . . and there are still farms in Indiana raising wholesome young women who grow up to work as double agents and look hot in red gowns.

Humanity's something else.

"The mission is clear," Phoebe says, her eyes cutting to me. "You obtain the asset. You pass it off to *me*. And then we take it from there."

Phoebe is on one side of the portal, glaring at me. I could go around the massive metal ring to get closer to her, but I opt instead to heft myself up the side. There's a metaphor in there, but I was never one for higher lit.

"What are you doing?" Phoebe demands. My eyes keep drifting to the bright strands of light weaving through her braided buns. I wonder if she wears her hair like that on purpose, to distract people from her eyes, from seeing what she sees. And she sees a lot.

"Relax, it's an interactive exhibit. I've been in here before when entire classrooms of children hung off this thing like it was a playground." All the rough edges of the portal have either been filed down, removed, or covered in protective foam so said schoolchildren don't get cut on the museum's dime. I have to hitch my sea-silk dress up a little, exposing almost my entire left thigh, before I get all the way up and settled onto the ring. With my legs stretched out in front of me, I lean my back against the inner curving metal of the ring, and I think about how a few hundred years ago, there were solar fuel cells built right below me, more energy than a hundred nuclear bombs, just simmering.

It's hollow and powerless now.

I loll my head toward Phoebe. At least my hair's so glued down, it's sturdier than the portal ring. "I know how the operation is supposed to work."

She narrows her eyes at me. "How it's *supposed* to work is exactly how it *will* work. You were hired for a job."

"I know," I say.

"And you're going to do that job."

I roll my eyes. *Believers.* She definitely feels she has a higher purpose, that her nobility counts for something.

"You're a lot like Fetor," I mumble. Everyone's trying to save the planet but only on their own terms.

Phoebe sputters at me, but before her affronted thoughts can gain any traction, I add, "That's why you can trust me. *I don't care about your little operation.* I care about getting paid."

"And the only way to *get* paid is to pass the asset off to me."

Oh, she's wrong about that. There are *lots* of ways to make a profit. Believers are never creative enough.

"The pass–off happens at the end of the night," I say as if that's a decade from now. As if it's that straightforward.

"We can't risk any delays."

I tap my fingers on the metal. There's a subtle, almost-indistinct hint of an echo, reminding me of how the portal's empty metal now. Reminding me that if this thing were in space still, even if it had no fuel cell core, it would make no sound at all.

"You do your job; I'll do mine," I say, locking eyes with her again. "I know what the stakes are."

"Do you?" There's an edge to her voice now, raw desperation. And I don't know if it's the hint of fear that flashes in her eyes or the way she really does look smoking in that dress, but I sit up a little straighter. Something breaks behind her pretty face when she sees that I'm actually paying attention.

"This is *it*," she says, her voice low but not because she thinks anyone can hear us. She knows this room is secure. Her voice is soft because she has so much hope pinned to her words that they're drowning her like pebbles stuffed in the pockets of a tragic Victorian about to walk into the sea. She takes a shaky breath in. "This is everything, *everything* that we've been planning for *years*. If you—"

"Get the asset," I fill in for her, "which I will."

"If you do, if this works . . . we might get Earth again. Real Earth. Not one dependent on tourism and charity. Climate sickness would be a thing of the past. Think of the people dependent on drugs just to keep living on our world."

Think of all the people not dependent on drugs, because living on our world already killed them. I silently state each word in my mind, and then I swallow them down, pushing the sentence deep into my gut, without letting a single syllable even float across my face.

She laughs, absolutely no amusement in her voice at all. "We might actually get the farm back."

"So to speak," I say.

"But if you fail—god, why does whole thing have to hinge on *you*?" She waves her hand at me as if I am the most inept person to ever breathe in her presence. Which is supremely fucking unfair, because just ten minutes ago, she saw Strom Fetor, who's *way* worse than me. I hope he falls off his hover stage during his big announcement.

"If you fail," Phoebe continues, utterly ignoring me as her eyes trace up to the part of the ceiling where the portal ring should continue but instead cuts off abruptly, "If you fail . . ."

"If I fail," I snark back, somewhat impatiently.

"Then the nanobots get released into Earth's climate, a Pandora's box that can never be closed. And when that happens, it will turn my world, *our* world into nothing more than a shell. He'll own us. All of us." She shakes her head.

This is exactly the kind of pressure I purposefully did not want to contemplate earlier. Yes, there's a hell of a lot riding on tonight.

The nanobots that were in the *Roundabout* were infected with code that will spread like a virus. Nanobots are designed to work that way, to replicate on their own, to infect everything. These nanobots are going into the water cycle, and every scientist in every world will confirm that the one essential thing to human life on a planet is a working water cycle.

Once released, the nanobots will be impossible to recapture.

The virus will spread.

And Earth will pay the price.

Quite literally. The nanobots are designed to cease

working, an encrypted code that Fetor purposefully designed to ensure he has to be rehired again and again. Rather than saving Earth, he's making every citizen sign up for a subscription plan that will bankrupt them, just for the privilege of staying alive.

"I know what you're thinking," Phoebe says.

You really, really don't, I think. But all I do is smile.

"You're thinking, well, Earth is dying. If this doesn't work, there's plenty of room on the other worlds. And it's true. People can immigrate. I'm sure that's what Fetor thinks. It's probably how he sleeps at night, telling himself that if people cannot afford to pay him to live, they can just move elsewhere."

"I'm sure he doesn't tell himself a damn thing at night, because if he does happen to have an ounce of empathy lingering like a stain on his conscious, he can just pay someone to have it removed."

Phoebe gives me a brief snort of appreciation at that, but then her face tilts, her mouth tightening, as if she's swallowing down acid. "It's just . . . not everyone can leave. He's going to own Earth, and he's going to own the people who can't afford to leave."

"I know," I say. Clear. Loud. Somewhat impatient.

But she's already drowning in her hope and her desperation. She can't hear anything I'm saying, not really.

I know what she's going through right now. This is the

first time the universe peeled away its veneer and showed her how cruel it can be, not out of any type of maliciousness but out of pure apathy. She's from Indiana, for fuck's sake; she's been a witness to horror, sure, but it's never before been hers to own.

And she doesn't know what to do with it all, except to keep trying to scramble over the waves, even if they slip through her fingers, even if she's using all her energy just to keep from going under.

She still thinks good can win. And she's not taken any of the stones out of her pockets yet.

But that crack in her voice, that thrum of anxiety wrapping around her neck, that tightening in her shoulders . . .

I swing my legs over the side of the portal, standing up close to her. I look her right in the eyes. I say: "I won't fail."

I see the moment when she chooses to believe in *me*.

And if there weren't so much profit on the line, I would pity her for that.

10

I head downstairs after that. Phoebe makes sure of it. Technically, guests are allowed to go wherever they want in the museum, but no one cares about the exhibits on regular display other than me. And Strom Fetor, I guess.

Phoebe leaves me when we're at the ground floor, but that doesn't mean I'm alone.

Most of the gala is in the auction rooms, but I no longer have a desire to see people bidding on scraps of Earth. This area here, in the back, is more interesting, especially now that I know the grand finale is going to be so elaborate. So ripe for failure.

I lean against the stone wall by the stairs, just watching.

Waiting.

Above, through the glass roof and the huge windows at the end of the corridor, there's enough lingering sunset through the giant panes of glass curving over the back of the museum to show the outline of the city beyond the carefully manicured lawn, but it's not yet dark enough for the ambient glow of millions of streetlights coming on to obliterate the pinprick stars peeking through the early night.

I get as close as I can to the black curtain to assess a little of what Phoebe's dealing with, but not close enough to make any of the waitstaff shoo me away. I get glimpses of the enormous control-panel system with five different people hovering over an array of switches and lit panels. Offline, Phoebe had said. This must control the elaborate hover stage Fetor wanted to use, as well the holographic display that will show people why we should trust a trillionaire to clean up Earth. Now that I know that's the plan, I can see the break in the black curtains, strategically positioned behind the clear acrylic platform and podium.

This is going to be dramatic. Someone boring will introduce Fetor, and then the curtain will part, and he'll rise over the crowd like a god, holographic displays illuminating everything.

I should be grateful—that's what Phoebe would say, and Rian, too. He's fucking pretentious, but this sort of spectacle will get the public interested. And fucking hell, I have to give Fetor credit, too. He perfectly orchestrated the protestors at the start of the gala to contrast brilliantly with this display—no wonder the holos the protestors used were so weak. This display? Going to blow that one out of the water. All the little technophiles are going to flock to Fetor, as usual, and this time, they'll support Sol-Earth's salvation instead of the latest data pad or overlays.

Making Fetor the face of the nanobots is going to sway public opinion for Earth. It's a good thing if he's in the spotlight right now, given how popular—for some god-awful reason—he is.

I don't have to like it, though.

I'll get my revenge when I replace the nanobot code he *wrote,* I think. Let him tower above the crowd, the king of rich assholes. He thinks he's announcing *his* nanobots, secretly designed to fail, designed to make him even wealthier.

The higher he rises, the more fun it'll be to watch him fall.

A burst of light draws my eyes to a new holo illumination. The words *FETOR TECH* in all caps shines over the black curtain.

"Not yet!" a rough voice shouts, loud enough for me to hear all the way from the sidelines, loud enough to make a server nearby jump, plates rattling. The holos cut off, and I blink away the blinding light. One of the techs hit the wrong switch too soon.

This little corner of the museum is backstage enough for me to watch the bland smiles of the servers drip off their faces when they turn away from the crowd. They head toward a door to the left of the colonnades, just past the black curtain and the flurry of activity happening there. I know from studying maps of the museum the door the waitstaff uses leads to an expansive area where all the real work happens—kitchens, conference rooms, offices. As I stand there, more workers emerge, removing the burnt-marshmallow seats and replacing them with rows of clear acrylic chairs.

Soon, everyone in the museum will be summoned here, to the main gallery hall, for the closing ceremony. Auction winners will be heralded. Fetor will announce that he's invented tech he didn't invent. Everyone will raise their glasses to him, and he'll smile and believe their cheers mean he's brilliant, and then the gala will end and everyone will go off to the real parties afterwards, and in the morning, the feeds will be splashed with vids of the best dressed, and maybe there will be a footnote about a planet that some people wish would just die so they didn't even have to pretend to care.

All I have to do is wait a little longer, and I can get off this world and back into the sky where at least people are honest when they lie.

And hopefully, I'll have the asset I was paid to acquire with me. Whether I do or not will dictate which direction I fly. But I've done all I can to lay the path.

Nothing to do but wait and see.

I stay in this spot long enough to track the players. The server with dark skin and long, vivid blue braids clocks me every time he walks by with an empty platter—always an empty platter. The security drone is on a scheduled loop, the lens flicking in my direction every fifteen minutes. A woman in a silver gown with a mirror-like finish has passed me three times on the way to the restroom, which is on the other side of the corridor. A flash of red across the hall— Phoebe's still keeping an eye on me. Rian's off with Fetor, but that doesn't mean I'm not watched.

Maybe I wouldn't have noticed the kid if I wasn't so busy noticing everyone else.

But I do see him. Young, maybe twenty if I'm generous, probably on the south side of eighteen or so. Golden eyes— fitted with holo specs. Medium-dark skin, silky black hair that brushes his shoulders. The ends are ragged, as if cut with blunt scissors.

He comes out the servers' door, slipping in between rows of workers pushing hovers loaded with stacks of straight-backed chairs. He's got a darty look about him, couldn't be more suspicious if he tried.

He doesn't notice me as he walks right past, up the stairs toward the second floor.

The server with blue hair dodges the chairs, his gaze flicking to me for a microsecond before pushing into the workers' door.

Rian's got everyone on his team watching me so hard, not a single other person has noticed the kid.

I spot the security drone, glimpse the silver dress.

And then turn on my heel and head up the stairs.

11

The kid is sitting right on the same step where Rian's hands gripped my hips so hard it would have hurt if it hadn't felt so good.

Kid's jumpy. Spots me a mile away, shoves something in his pocket.

Fucking great.

Sometimes, I hate when I'm right.

I walk up the steps slowly, mindful of my dumb shoes. I stop two steps below the kid, wait for him to look up at me.

Those wide golden eyes flick up to me, the lenses of his specs dilating and narrowing again. Bet he's got some processor linked in. There's a tiny bump behind his left ear—a subcutaneous receiver that's perfectly positioned for bone-conduction audio. His specs have scanned my face, and the receiver is reading him information no one but him can hear.

It's good tech. Better than what I have, usually.

Good tech isn't abnormal here. The fucking protestors that were paid by the hour had better stuff than I can afford, and they didn't even have an invite into this shindig. No, the level of tech's not off.

It's his clothes.

You can fake fancy clothes. Happens all the time, especially on a planet that cares more about people's appearance than their welfare.

When it comes to rich people, you can always tell by the clothes. It's not a matter of style or flashiness, no. It's a matter of quality. My dress is simple, but it's made of sea-silk. Poly fibers could have the exact same coloring, but it wouldn't have flowed the same way over my skin. While I bought it pre-made, it was altered to my measurements, designed for my body.

This kid's suit was an afterthought. A disguise.

But not his tech.

That's the key thing. That's the thing to notice.

"Hey," I say.

"Fuck off," the kid says.

"Nice."

"The party's downstairs."

"Is it?"

That catches him up. I've got probably ten minutes before Rian's people notice I'm not somewhere in the crowd, maybe fifteen before they actively start looking for me. Kid doesn't know that, though.

"What do you want?" he demands.

I hike my dress up a little so I can sit down on the step beside him, leaning my back against the wall, my head almost brushing the underside of the railing as I face the kid. I take a long breath through my nostrils, let it out through my red-lacquered lips. "Don't do it," I say.

His jaw twitches. "I'm just sitting here," he says. And then, "Mind your business."

I stretch my legs out on the steps. "No."

"No?" his voice rises. He's new to this.

"No," I repeat. "Because you're about to fuck everything up, and I'm going to stop you before you do."

"The fuck do you know, old woman?"

Okay, that was uncalled-for. Rude. I lick my teeth, making a smacking noise.

"Listen here, you little fuck," I say. "If you think you're the only one who's noticed there's no security drones in this corner of the stairwell, you're dumber than you look."

He blanches, his skin going a little splotchy, but his shoulders roll back. This one's all vinegar and piss, and he just wants a fight, no matter what.

Reminds me of me.

So, I forgive him for being a smartass and turn away so he can save a little face. "Came in through the back door," I say. "Headed straight here. Better tech than you're used to."

I give him a sidelong glance, notice the way he twitches again. That box in his pocket's burning a hole right through him. "Jarra?"

"No," he snarls immediately.

Yes. He's working with the Jarra. Those fuckers like to do this sort of thing.

Sending a kid in for sacrifice.

The gala tonight has too good of security for brute force short of open warfare to work. Even the airspace above the building's regulated. No drone in here that's not attached directly to security. A good chunk of the guests with private bodyguards, another chunk undercover.

But this is a gala to benefit Earth. A charity fundraiser.

And while the Jarra are also from Earth, they're not a group that really likes charity or benefits. This is exactly the shit they hate. They don't want help from other worlds. They want Earth to separate from the United Galactic; they want everyone who's chosen to leave the homeworld to stay gone.

I'd bet my dress the Jarra know of Fetor's announcement, of the nanobots that are supposed to come and save everyone. More meddling from off-worlders, tied to the government at that. I know for a fact they hate Fetor on principle for all the shit he pulled with the vaccine rollout for climate sickness a decade ago; they wouldn't mind taking him out and making a political statement against government intervention at the same time.

I glance at the kid. He's too jumpy to be an assassin.

But he's stupid enough to be a bomb.

"Give me your transponder," I say, holding my hand out without looking directly at him.

"No," he snaps. Then, "I don't have a transponder."

Fucking idiot. "What did they tell you?" I sigh.

He glares at me, lips sealed.

"What's your exit plan?" I ask softly, turning back to face him.

His expression is all tight jaw and tense neck.

"Just going to do a runner?" I guess.

The barest hint of a shrug, mostly unconscious but a little bit testing the waters.

The Jarra would know that any attack on the gala would be a suicide mission. They never intended for the kid to escape. They never even pretended to give him a way out. But I bet they told him he could make a run for it in the chaos.

See, this is why I will *never* work for those assholes.

Because they think killing Fetor is worth killing this kid. Make no mistake. This gala is crawling with security, and it's not all here for me. Whatever stunt this kid pulls, he *will* get caught.

And they didn't even tell him that.

I hold my hand out and snap my fingers.

"I don't have anything," the kid insists, a hint of whine creeping into his voice.

"Listen, kid, you're going to fuck up both my and your plans if you don't just hand it over."

"Your plans?" he asks, his hand moving unconsciously to his pocket. Finally.

Here's the thing. Rian has to have files and files and files on the Jarra. And I'm sure, at the top, those files are important. But the people at the top? They don't get their hands dirty. Or blown off.

That's what they use kids for.

I wonder how many plans go awry because they let young idiots who think they know what they're fighting for carry them. An event like this? It's a shot in hell that it'll go anywhere. But then again—

Quantity over quality, that's the Jarra. This isn't the only shindig in the galaxy. I bet they sent kids out to a dozen different places, scattered over all the colonial worlds. Some of them will get caught by the law. Some of them will get caught in the crossfire.

But all they care about is what gets caught on camera. And something, no doubt, will filter through.

It's a numbers game.

Gentle chimes echo throughout the museum. Bids are closed. People have fifteen minutes before the final show begins.

On the one hand, that's a distraction. I can already hear the ambient noise of all the guests trickling from the auction rooms into the main gallery, where the chairs are lined in perfectly spaced rows and a hover stage has been set up, waiting for Fetor.

On the other hand, that's only fifteen minutes before this kid wants to do an entirely different show.

12

His fingers itch to get out the transponder he thinks he's cleverly hidden in his pocket. He still thinks there's a chance I'll just walk away and let him play the big-boy games.

"Hey, kid, do you know Jane—" I start.

"Don't fucking try to recruit me to some weak-ass group not willing to do what it really takes to make change," he snarls.

Okay, touched a sore spot there. I level him with a look. "Nothing I can do to stop you, huh?"

His grin is smug. That's a *no*, then.

I tap the stone step with my fingernail, thinking. "Let me tell you how to run a con."

He stares at me as if I've lost my mind, the smirk melting away in his confusion at my non sequitur.

"You want to steal something? You could be a ghost, but that'll only work for so long. Eventually, you're going to find someone who sees you."

Someone with razor eyes.

"And when you're seen," I continue, "you have to change tactics. You have to do it all in front of everyone."

The kid's smirk twitches up again. I was right. He's desperate to not be invisible. But he doesn't get it, not yet.

I lean in closer. "Part one. Distract." I waggle my fingers in front of his face with my left hand, reach for his pocket with my right.

He grabs my wrist, fingers hard, digging into the soft space over my veins, pressing into the tiny, thin bones. "I'm not that dumb."

"Doubt that," I say, yanking my hand free. "Besides, part two. You can steal anything in the galaxy if you make people think it's their idea to give it to you in the first place."

He rakes his eyes over me, not trying to hide his disgust. "You don't talk like one of them."

One of the elite, he means.

"Because I'm not, moron." But he's wrong. I may not be used to wearing silk and gems, but I learned how to steal from people like those in the crowd below. This kid just doesn't realize that people like Fetor get what they want because they've convinced people like him it's their right. "I'm from Earth," I say. "Like you."

"Why do you even care what I'm doing, then?" Sullen and petulant; what a charmer.

I shrug. "Not a big fan of things going boom." At least, not when I'm not the one holding the detonator.

"I'm not doing anything like that," he says, shaking his head so much, his hair flops around.

I lift an eyebrow so high, Rian would be proud.

That thought sends a chill down my spine. If Rian strolls up these steps, he's going to think I'm working with the kid.

"Wait," I say, shaking my head and refocusing. If the transponder's not linked to explosives—the usual Jarra MO . . . "What's the transponder for?"

He finally pulls it out, done pretending. "I'm just messing with the holo display."

Aw, that's cute. I got started the same way, hacking digi screens to send a message.

The chimes clang again, a little louder. *Time to take your seats,* they say. *The show is starting soon.*

It's just . . .

The kid's definitely working with the Jarra. This plan has got their bloody fingerprints all over it. "If you're just hacking the show, let me see the transponder," I say.

His holo specs whirr. By now, I bet they've pulled up a file on me, and this kid is hearing about my stunt a few years back, the messed-up ad sys.

Who better to appreciate his stunt than someone who knows code?

He shrugs like he doesn't care about what's going to happen next. The kid shoves the black box into my waiting hands. There's a lift to his chin.

He's proud of this, of himself. That's how the Jarra get ones like him. Find the kids who are mad, make them feel important. Promise them recognition only when the job is done. This kid's desperate for someone—*anyone*—to see him, *really* see him. He wants to light a spark just so someone will see him in the dark.

But it's not safe to play with fire, not when you don't know how deep the burns can go.

"Where you from?" I ask, flipping the box over.

"Austral— Wait, don't do that!"

I flick open the back with my fingernail and look at the circuitry inside. Kid didn't make this transponder; it's too neat. Every part here was bought with purpose, not scrapped together.

I tap my cuff against the receiver, activating the wireless programming I keep ready. This wouldn't work for anything much more complicated, but scanning code isn't hard.

"Here, hold this," I say, tossing the black lid of the transponder to the kid as I reach inside my reticule and pull out my small data pad, linking it through my cuff to the transponder. In moments, info flashes on the screen.

"What are you—" he starts, leaning closer.

It's just code, and my eyes skim over the illuminated series of commands. For all the advancements in the universe, it's kind of amazing how simple code can be, how we can cross the galaxy at light speed with binary, using the same string of commands that made that clunky red telephone upstairs.

This is a light show. Linked up to the holos that are going to be on display.

Downstairs, I hear a female voice call for attention over the loudspeakers. She's thanking the gala attendees and announcing how much has been raised for Sol-Earth. I can almost visualize her on the acrylic stage, gesturing grandly behind the clear podium, the black curtain behind her just waiting to part.

"Give that back," the kid demands.

"You're not activating shit until Fetor starts talking," I say, still reading the code. It's all linked to the display Fetor's going to give—holo projections of Earth.

And—

There it is.

Right after the display announces Fetor's saved Earth with his nanobots, which will be released soon.

"You code this?" I ask the kid.

"Yeah." He's all chuffed.

I tilt the screen to him. "You code *all* this?"

His eyes scan the screen. He pauses. I watch his lenses contract to pinpricks. He points to where the code starts to go awry. "What's—"

"That's the part where things go boom."

He snatches the screen on my data pad, scrolling through

it. My grip is tight around the transponder, even though he doesn't reach for it again.

It's clever coding, I'll give them that. It starts off with nothing more than a prank—that's the kid's writing; I can see the clunky style of it. The holos were going to showcase the nanobots, and the code is linked to make them display a mockery, swarming the holo representations of the bots into an obscene body part pointed at Fetor's head. I can honestly appreciate that bit.

Seamlessly wrapped around that code, though, is something more insidious.

Every single element of tonight's event has had to go past security, through scanners, and beyond the careful eye of Rian and his people. Any physical bomb would have been caught.

With all the live feeds that will surely be pointed at the "glitching" holos, that's going to be a lot of eyes when the hover stage Strom Fetor is on explodes.

"That was a smart touch," I say. Credit where it's due.

"What?" The kid's voice is all hollow. He's starting to realize how deep he's in the shit.

"There's no bomb, no explosives. You just programmed the hover to overload and ignore the failsafes." Nothing to smuggle in except a transponder—that's how they got past all the security. The transponder's innocuous on its own; if anyone did bother to check the kid's pockets, it wouldn't have triggered anything or shown up on any scanner. And there's nothing to detect on the stage itself. I'm certain Rian had it examined a million times. There was nothing for him to find except some override code in a kid's pocket.

We had to take Fetor's tech offline, Phoebe said before. They needed the kid on site to activate with a transponder; the Jarra couldn't hack into a system not on the network. Slip in the code to make the stage itself fail, and bam. Fireworks. The deaths of Strom Fetor and anyone who happened to be beneath the stage caught on live feed, broadcast to trillions of people across all four worlds.

"I . . ." The kid's voice trails off.

And I get it. I do. Fetor blowing up on stage in front of a lot of live feeds is . . .

Kind of appealing; not gonna lie.

But it'll fuck up all my plans.

The kid's hacking means the whole stage will overheat to catastrophic levels soon after Fetor starts speaking, and the stage will literally crash and burn—which, again, is a chef's-kiss level of awesome if only it didn't mean that (a) some innocents below would get hurt too, and (b) I have bigger metaphorical fish to metaphorically fry than literally frying Strom Fetor.

I sigh. I'm going to have to stop this from happening. "Murdering the richest man in the galaxy on live feeds? You'll never escape."

His eyes go wide. "I've gotta get out of here now," he says. "I have a family—my mom . . ." His voice cracks, and that cracks at my own little shriveled heart. Boys always want their mommas when they realize they fucked up.

I grab the back of the transponder and put it back on the box, careful not to push the big red button that will emit the transmission that will overwrite the failsafes of the hover stage. I keep a tight grip on the box, though; no way am I letting the kid have it back. "It's fine," I say, placating him. "Just don't start the sequence. Go down, steal some good food, go home, and quit working for assholes who think you're disposable."

He shakes his head, hair whipping around his face. "You don't understand," he says all in a rush, eyes wide. "I already pushed the button. The sequence is *already* timed and programmed. I heard your shoes on the steps—I pushed the button then, before you got up to me. It's already overwritten the code in the stage. As soon as Fetor starts speaking, the holos are going to change, and then . . ."

And then boom.

13

Well, fuck.

The kid's eyes are wild. He signed up for a prank, not murder.

Gentle waves of clapping from downstairs. Auction winners lauded for spending money. Almost time for the finale.

"I've gotta get out of here," the kid says. All that false bravado has turned into panic. His only chance now is distance. Before I can wrap my head around just how bad this is, he's bounding down the steps. I could chase him down, or I can figure this out.

Don't get me wrong; Strom Fetor exploding on stage is absolutely appealing, and I would normally pay cash money for a front-row seat to that. Well, considering how the stage is now programmed to crash directly into the audience, maybe not *front*-row.

But I *need* my dominos to fall just right.

Fuck. Dropping the evidence in my bag, the silk purse now showing sharp corners, I head downstairs in time to see the staff door swinging from where the kid made his escape. My eyes dart across the room. If I can flag down one of the people who was supposed to be watching me, let them know the stage is going to explode before the show's over . . .

Where the fuck is everyone?

I stick close to the wall, creeping behind the black curtain. The command center for the stage and holo displays and live feeds is along the far wall. There are more workers here, bustling prep for the finale, but there's no red dress or blue hair to spot me. There's no Rian.

Only Strom Fetor.

He catches my eye and grins. He's already on the stage, a narrow platform with a little lip in front.

If I had half an hour and a code splicer, I could work around the kid's hack.

But I don't.

If I go over to the impromptu command center they've set up and tell them the problem, would they believe me?

Maybe.

"Let's hear it for the auction winners!" the female voice of the presenter calls from her position on the acrylic stage on the other side of the curtain. Fetor steps forward, depressing a button hidden under the front lip of the hover stage. It slowly rises in the air, about thirty or forty centimeters, not too high. Lights spark under the hover stage, the holos already warming up. I remember then what Phoebe said earlier, about how this tech stage is a new prototype. I wonder if Fetor would get the blame if I let those holos overheat and he smashes into the crowd below. Actually, a pretty smart hack—but also another reason why people would then call into question whether or not the nanobots to clean Earth should be used.

The presenter on the other side of the curtain says, "And now, let me introduce the man of the hour!"

So much for the easy way out.

I start running. The grand corridor is wide, but even with my shit shoes, it takes me only a few minutes to reach Fetor. I can feel people backstage watching me, curious about the woman darting across the hall, but they probably think I'm on some errand or something. No one stops me when I reach the stage, and no one, especially not Fetor, expected me to dive at it. I feel the slit in my dress rip as I scramble up.

"What are you doing?" Fetor whisper-shouts at me.

"Houston, we have a problem," I mutter.

The presenter is still droning on about how awesome Fetor is, and fuck, do I hope, for once, that she'll keep at it. I see guards now, uniformed security heading straight toward us, but at least I can get a sense of the controls from here. The stage is designed to be remotely operated—that's what the command center is for—but some simple directional buttons are built into the base. I stomp on the big red arrow labelled *up*, and Fetor and I lift from the ground, almost to the top of the black curtain, well beyond the jumping grasps of the security guards below.

The stage judders, dropping a dozen centimeters in a stomach-whooshing movement that makes Fetor curse and stumble. The command center. They operate the stage remotely. I step on the *Lock* button, the abrupt stop putting us still well beyond the security guards' reach.

Outside, the crowd titters in polite laughter at something the presenter said. Her intro has to be winding down now. And no one of the other side of the curtain knows that I've hijacked Fetor's stage.

"The show is starting; get off!" Fetor says, reaching for me. The platform's not that big, only wide enough for five or so people to stand if they don't mind not having much elbow room. He grabs for my arm, but as soon as he touches me, I yank away. What's he going to do, shove me off stage? At this height, I could break a leg.

I skim the faces at the command center, settling on one man glaring at me, the only person not moving among a flurry of frantic workers.

Rian. His eyes slice right to me.

"Get off!" Fetor says, louder. Loud enough that maybe the people in the audience can hear.

I stomp his foot with my stiletto heel, and Fetor yelps in pain. Finally, those stupid shoes prove worthwhile. I ignore

Fetor entirely, my focus on Rian, as I lift my hands, my reticule swinging, bulky with the kid's transponder inside. Rian's had space training. I have to hope . . .

Do you trust me? I sign, beseeching him with my eyes to understand the stakes have changed, the game's different now.

He shakes his head frantically, and then, just in case I didn't get the picture, signs, *Absolutely not, whatever you're planning, absolutely NOT.* His hands are in such a flurry, I can barely comprehend them, but the gist is clear.

I shrug. Well, I tried.

With a wink at Rian, I kneel on the platform. On the other side of the curtain, the audience's clapping grows louder. Seconds now. I scan the wiring, sending a prayer of thanks up that this stage is a prototype. Behind the lip at the front, the wiring is still exposed. Hell, maybe the kid *didn't* need to hack the stage; this thing really is not well designed. There's a distinct smell of burning ozone. The kid said the hack wouldn't overheat the holos until later in the speech, but I don't trust that to hold true.

"And now!" the presenter calls over the claps of the audience. "Our guest of honor, Strom Fetor!"

Here goes nothing.

I tangle my fingers in the wires and yank a handful of blue and red and purple and white, ripping them out.

"What the—" Fetor starts.

And the stage smashes down.

Fetor and I both go sprawling, the wind knocked out of us, but I'm sensible enough to appreciate that the guards who'd been trying to grab for us are unharmed, if dazed and shocked.

For one split second, the entire museum is silent, the reverberations of the crash behind stage fading. This was *loud*. The audience didn't know Strom was going to fly out from behind the curtain like a god, but that cacophony didn't sound planned.

Then the noise picks up. The guards rush the cracked remains of the stage, grabbing and pulling me bodily away. Someone's shouting. I see more people run to Fetor, who's already standing up and brushing off his jacket, his face purple with rage. Some people dressed to the nines talk frantically to him, and there's a grim set to his jaw. The presenter is trying to calm the concerned audience, and some people— likely with the museum—rush from that side to this side of the curtain.

And then the guards slam me through the employee entrance. Waitstaff go scattering.

"In here," one of them says, and I'm shoved into a conference room.

I get just one line from Fetor, his voice amplified over the noise and chaos. "Folks, sorry about that loud crash," he says. He must have walked through the curtain and taken the clear stage after I broke his toy. I get part of his next sentence: "Tonight's all about history, so I shouldn't be surprised the museum couldn't handle some of my newer technology!"

There's a wave of relieved laughter. They're all going to pretend nothing happened.

The conference room door slams, sealing me inside. I kick off my shoes—hateful things—and sling myself into one of the leather swivel chairs at the table, releasing all the pent-up adrenaline as my body melts into the seat.

Well, that could have gone better.

14

The conference room door bangs open so abruptly that I jump. Rian storms inside.

"Hello," I say cheerily.

Another man follows him in, then slams the door shut again. He has tightly coiled white hair over an ashen face and a grim expression. The infamous Jacques Winters, gala director.

Outside, Fetor's got to be at least ten minutes into his little speech. Had I not done what I did, there would have been a lot more screaming and a lot fewer inane jokes played for polite laughter.

"Ada, what the *fuck*," Rian snarls.

"Okay, you're mad," I say.

Rian glowers at me, jaw tight, but the white-haired man whirls on him. "You *know* her?"

Rian doesn't even look at him. His eyes burn into me. "Why?" he chokes out.

In answer, I reach for my purse. The white-haired man jumps, but Rian holds out a hand, ready to take what I'm offering.

My data pad.

I flip it on, unlock the screen, and bring up the kid's hack. "By the time I caught him, he'd already set the command into motion," I say, also handing over the transponder.

"What is it?" Winters asks, looking at the screen.

Shit. Rian doesn't know code. Winters doesn't seem to, either, but another man enters the conference room—the blue-haired server. He takes the data pad from Rian, and the two of them quickly confer. I let them talk. I shoot Winters a charming smile, but it doesn't make his scowl lessen. Tough crowd.

Rian turns to me, looking across the room from his position by the door. "Who—"

I cut him off. "The Jarra."

The gala director whips around to me. Finally an expression from him other than rage. "You intercepted something from the Jarra?"

"Hi." I beam at him. "My name's Ada Lamarr, and tonight I saved your ass. In front of all the live feeds, too. You are welcome."

"You intercepted a terrorist?" Rian said, ignoring my polite introductions. The blue-haired man leaves.

I stopped a kid from fucking up his own life, I think. I could care less what happened to Fetor. But that kid was never going to get away with what he'd done.

"Where is—" Winters looks around as if the entirety of

the underground movement were standing in the conference room, weapons drawn.

"He's gone," I say casually.

"Gone?" Rian narrows his eyes.

"I took care of it."

His brows wrinkle; his jaw tightens.

"Speaking of." I turn to the coordinator, shooting him a smile. "I did promise Fetor that red telephone from the Mission Control display as an apology for messing up his fancy speech." A lie, but a believable one.

His eyes widen. "That was not yours to—"

"Yeah, obviously. But consider how stopping your own guest of honor's hover stage from turning into a raging inferno of death and destruction may have saved you a little face."

"Why didn't you alert the authorities?" the coordinator shouts.

"I tried." I look at Rian, raising my hands and making the signs for *Do you trust me?* A little muscle near his left eye tics. I turn my full attention to the coordinator. "But time was of the essence, and the show must go on, no?"

Winters looks at his cuff band, eyes bouncing off glowing letters as ping after ping swamps the receiver. "I need to—"

Rian waves him off without taking his eyes off me. He pulls out a chair, sitting down as the coordinator leaves us alone, the door clicking shut behind us.

I lean forward before Rian can speak. "I didn't do this," I say, jerking my head toward the data pad without breaking eye contact. "I came across a kid who got conned into delivering a hack." Outside, we can hear Fetor's speech echoing throughout the museum. He's not physically lifted above the crowd; there are no glittering displays. But I catch the word *nanobots*, and the resulting cheers from the audience make me reasonably sure things are going well.

A soft knock on the door. Rian stands to open it. The woman in the silver dress. I hear them muttering for a moment, catching things like "drone footage confirms" and "there did seem to be a breach through the staff hall." She hands Rian a huge, padded bag. Rian shuts the door again when she leaves.

Inside the black bag is a plethora of devices. Rian sets them up on the conference table, ignoring me when I lean forward to look. He's checking up on my story, checking all the security drones, linking in to the transponder to see what else it has. I let him work for a while.

I let him prove my story correct.

"Look," I say once I'm certain he knows I wasn't lying, at least not about this, "cards on the table. I did *not* wake up this morning intending to bump into some kid recruited for the Jarra and have to fuck up all his plans to make way for my own."

"A kid?" Rian's face softens, then goes tense again. "But what were your plans?"

I shrug. "You won't believe me. But . . . I've got a little bit of a track record going for me," I say, quieter. "No one dies. Even if that messes up my own agenda."

Oh, that's eating him up inside. Because it's true. Last time we crossed paths, the last words I said to him were claiming that no one died in the crash of the UGS *Round-about,* and I have no doubt that he followed up on that, proving me right. And the evidence of the kid's hack is right there in front of him.

"You could be working with—"

"No." My harsh word cuts him off. "No," I repeat, just as strongly. I let out a breath through my nose. "We all have our lines we don't cross."

Rian puts the data pad on the table, scooting his chair close to mine. Our knees bump. It reminds me of being in the shuttle with him, exploring the protoplanet where the *Roundabout* crashed, telling him truths and lies and waiting to see which ones he believed.

"What other lines do you have, Ada?" he asks. His voice is low, rough.

I shrug, and while my face is casual, my tone matches his. "Very few. Limits aren't really my thing."

Eyebrow arch. "I can see that."

My hands move from my lap to his knees, my fingers pressing against his firm thighs. I stand, the chair scooting behind me, but I keep my face even with his, my hands on him, my body angled so that I fill his vision. "As far as dates go, this one has been pretty terrible, but there's still time for you salvage it."

It takes a few minutes for my words to process in his head. He snorts. "This isn't a date, Ada." He's working so hard to keep his eyes on mine, not drifting south. What a gentleman.

"It could be," I whisper. "And what an exciting story it would become."

He scoots back in his chair, pushing my hands away. I straighten up, using this opportunity to look down at him. He picks up my data pad.

"I'm keeping this," he says.

"Then you're going to reimburse me," I snap back.

"Consider the data recorder you stole from *Halifax* to be payment."

"That was a gift," I say.

"The information on it wasn't."

Fine. He's not bending on that.

I slip my shoes back on—they're painful, but the tile floor is cold. "The gala's almost over," I say. "Show a girl a good time."

He's going to let me off the hook for the stage shenanigans. I know it; he knows it. Everything he's checked has proven my story. Rian knew that part of the stairs was the only blind spot, but he's retroactively tracked the kid's entry and exit, and he sees the evidence I've gathered. When some expert analyzes the code, maybe they'll even be able to trace it back to some member of the Jarra who set the kid up, I don't know. But it's pretty obvious now that I stopped a much bigger crisis from happening, and whether he likes it or not, Rian's going to forgive me for the little stunt I pulled.

And it's been enough to distract him from what I actually came here to steal.

15

Rian's not letting me out of his sight again; that's for damn sure. He escorts me to the now-dark windows at the back of the main gallery, and we watch on screens as Fetor finishes up his speech on the other side of the black curtain.

"Backstage at the biggest event of the year," I say. "I feel like a VIP."

"I feel like I can't let you out of my sight."

"You're such a flirt."

"Trust me, folks," Fetor says on stage, the voice amp picking up his resonant chuckle. "We had a great display set up for you to explain it all, but—"

Rian notices the way my lips snarl. "Why do you hate Strom Fetor so much?" His voice is low, and we're far enough away from others that our conversation is, essentially, private.

"Do I need a reason?" I ask. "He's so hateable, on so many levels."

"Is Fetor the reason why you're here?" Rian tries to keep

this all business. He's so focused on me, he doesn't even notice the way Phoebe is on the other side of the hallway, whispering to a tall man with reddish-brown skin and crinkly eyes, both of whom keep looking at us conspiratorially. I wish there was a way I could eavesdrop on the office gossip that I am absolutely thrilled to be in the center of with Rian. From their point of view, I was caught making out with Rian and then escaped certain punishment after that stunt on the hover stage, and now I'm hanging off his arm. I slither a little closer to him, and it takes him a full five seconds for him to move his hand when it brushes against my hip.

"I didn't come here for Fetor," I say. Lie. The job I was hired to do had nothing to do with Fetor, but part of the reason I accepted it had everything to do with it. Dominos. Still, to Rian's face, I say, "I consider personally informing Fetor that I despise every molecule in his body as a bonus of the job. Almost better than the food. It would also have been a bonus if he'd caught on fire in front of a live audience, but I had to improvise on that one. You're welcome."

"Thank you," Rian mutters, but he doesn't sound grateful at all. "So, Strom wasn't your job?"

"Of course he's not," I say. Someone closer to the stage glances back at us, glowering, as if she's far more concerned about what Fetor has to say than anything else, which is just ridiculous.

"But then why do you hate him?" Rian asks, softer.

"Do I need a reason?"

"Just curious."

"I don't think anyone should have enough personal wealth to decimate a large country's income just because he's going through a midlife crisis."

Rian frowns, considering. There are at least three things I could be referring to with that statement. The bureaucratic coup that shifted control of the communications network from Fetor's mother to Fetor himself also saw a shift of the main office from Centauri-Earth to Rigel-Earth, creating an economic crisis on the former. Fetor's brief, passing interest in ship development saw him purchase and then bankrupt the largest engine manufacturing chain, which resulted in alternative fuel systems all but disappearing from sale.

And that's not even mentioning . . .

"Your father," Rian says softly, razor-blade gaze on me, cutting off every mask I usually wear.

I nod tightly, not trusting myself to talk.

See, Fetor's family wealth did start on Earth, and while his family's compound in the heart of the United Russo-Asian Republic may have been vastly different from my own upbringing in rural America, that little bit of shared homeworld would normally garner my sympathy.

Not for Fetor.

"I thought you'd appreciate the climate-sickness vaccine," Rian says.

"I do." I wrap my arms around my shoulders, unconsciously touching the rough patch of skin near my left underarm. The med patch vaccine left a scar, one anyone who was in the first few years of vaccines has. They have a milder version now, one that doesn't leave a mark.

Climate sickness only affects people on Earth. Radiation and pollution combined into a lethal outcome for hundreds of thousands of people before anyone even started to try to find a cure, and it was only in factories like Fetor's, ones that were literally on the planet, that there was any sort of concentrated effort to discover a cure, even if other planets claimed to offer help.

Fetor's medical research facilities discovered the vaccine and treatments to help those already sick first. I'll give him that. The researchers saved billions of lives.

But not at first.

At first, after the trials and experiments, the only people who got the vaccine or treatment were those who could afford it.

"Eight years," I say, my eyes blurring as the audience starts to clap for Fetor. The show's about to end.

Rian touches my shoulder. When I release my hold on myself, I see the lingering traces of my handprints on my arms.

"Eight years of profit before he sold the patent to the government. Three more years before the government was able to manufacture enough vaccines and distribute them widely. Eleven years, total, before anyone who wanted the meds got them." I don't look at him. "A lot can happen in eleven years."

"Thank you, thank you!" Fetor shouts into the amp as gold and silver confetti falls from the ceiling over the crowd. The audience roars in approval.

While the kid hacked into the holo display of the hover stage, there are permanent display holos built into the museum's network. The holo projection of Sol-Earth that illuminates and reflects through the metallic confetti is safe, although I expect Winters to have triple-checked to ensure it wasn't sabotaged as well. Music swells as the projection of the planet slowly twirls midair.

Not Earth as it is now, no, but as it was centuries ago. White at the caps. Blue in the oceans, green in the land. No bubbles of protection over specific landmarks. No America broken by plates shifting after the supervolcano erupted. No garbage island in the Pacific, so dense that it's now inhabited by bands of independent rovers.

Earth as it was.

As it will never be again, even with all the money of all the people in this room.

I glance at the O-ring pinned to Rian's rose corsage. Sometimes, when something breaks, it stays broken.

Rian's not watching the people. He's watching me.

"It takes time to distribute medical care to every inhabitant of a planet," he says. "In the history books, it's considered a miracle that in just a little more than a decade, everyone had access to a life-saving treatment."

I nod silently. Then I say, "How much of that time was wasted on haggling over the sale price of the patent on the vaccine?"

He doesn't answer.

One thing both Fetor and Rian have in common is this deep desire to save the world. Fetor wants the credit. Rian just wants to do good.

But . . . I don't need to save the whole world.

I just needed to save my father.

And he didn't have eleven years to wait.

The museum coordinator strides past us, and I startle. I was so lost in my own thoughts, I almost forgot about the purpose of the chaos around us. Winters mounts the acrylic stage in front of the black curtain, waving his hand for attention from both Fetor and the audience. "It has been our joy to host you tonight, and I must extend my deepest gratitude for our guest of honor, Strom Fetor!" The cheering from the audience gets even louder, and servers pop up, glasses of fizzy wine on silver platters.

"You know, the climate-cleaner nanobots that we're rolling out . . . they're nothing like the vaccine distribution." Rian tugs on my arm, pulling my attention to him. I blink rapidly, refocusing. "Maybe the climate-sickness vaccine could have been distributed more efficiently. But this is different."

"Because you're in charge?"

He flinches at the bitter bite of my words. "Because it's already in motion." He turns me away from the stage, enclosing me in our private conversation. "I don't know what the people you're working for told you, but what you stole from the *Roundabout* crash? It delayed us, but it didn't stop us. You took a prototype on its way to the final stage of testing and development, and while we had to recreate the data and send an entirely new one to the facility, you did nothing more than hold up production."

There's an accusation in his voice, an undercurrent of blame that makes bile rise in my throat. *If Fetor's family made Earth wait more than a decade for climate sickness treatment,* Rian's saying in his tone, *how are you any better for delaying climate cleaners from spreading all across the planet?*

I want to tell him everything.

Not yet, though. Not here.

Instead, I say, "I know."

I pull a tube out of my reticule and slick shiny gloss over my red-stained lips.

The museum coordinator makes a motion, and a woman crosses to the stage, a black box in her arms. When Fetor lifts the lid, he grins in delight, showing the red telephone from Mission Control to the audience, who—somehow—cheers even louder.

Rian's voice is so soft that I almost miss his words in the cacophony around us. "What do you know, Ada Lamarr?"

I lean close to him, tugging on his shoulder so I can whisper in his ear. "More than you," I say, and then, before he can pull away, I let the tip of my tongue dart out and lick the shell of his ear, just so I can watch him try not to unravel at the galaxy's biggest event of the year.

16

The fizzy wine is flowing, and while some groups are starting to break up, the party is still going strong.

Which only makes Rian jumpier.

He keeps waiting for me to make a break for it. It's like he still thinks I might try to cram Pharaoh Tutankhamun's liver into my purse, but he must have realized by now there's more at play here than that.

"Dessert?" a server says, pausing in front of us with a tray full of delights.

"No, thank you," I say.

Rian's eyes grow wide. "Are you okay?" he gasps, incredulous as I watch the tiny plates of chocolate-covered berries walk away. He frowns in concern.

Part of me wants to shove him aside, race to the server, and shovel the chocolate into my mouth by the fistful.

But the part of me that wants to get paid wins out. So, rather than follow the absolutely logical course of action, I turn my back on the food.

He's watching me even closer now. Maybe he can sense

the anticipation coiling in my gut like a snake. He's always so observant, my Rian.

So, I pick a fight.

"Did you really think I wouldn't notice?" I ask, eyes flicking down to his jacket.

"Notice?" Rian's brow creases.

I jab the O-ring he's used to affix the rose to his lapel. "I told you something real and true, and this is what you choose to make a mockery of?"

It takes him a moment to follow—good; I hope that means he forgot about the dessert thing. But once he finally pieces together my accusation, he blanches.

"You think I'm making fun of an entire family that died due to a ship malfunction?" he asks, reaching for the corsage. He shakes his head, and some of his carefully slicked-back hair breaks free. "No, no, that's not what this is."

"Oh, yeah?" I cross my arms, glaring at him, but inside, my heart leaps. I hadn't actually thought he was making light of such a horrific event, but I had thought he was mocking *me*. From his tone, though, I can tell I missed whatever point he was truly trying to make.

"It's to remind me that something small makes all the difference in the world," he says softly. He's looking at me, right into my eyes, all earnest and soulful, and it's making my knees melt like the chocolate I wish was on my tongue.

"Oh?" I say, trying to yank myself back into the here and now.

He nods. "I made a mistake once."

"Just the once?"

That gets me a smirk. "I saw someone who I *knew* was trouble."

"Can't be me, then."

"And rather than believe she was as capable as she said, I overlooked just how much damage she could do."

"She sounds like my type."

"Ada."

I mocked him once for the way he said my name, voice deep and serious. And I want to mock him again, now, except—

Except now it's not just my knees that are melting, it's all of me going liquid, all of me burning, all of me longing. Wanting.

My name forms on his lips, and it throws me right back into the past, to that moment where I let myself pretend, for one night, that I could have a life like the one he thinks he wants. He told me he liked the idea of knowing where I was in the universe, but he's a goddamn liar, because I can see the truth painted all over his flushed skin. He says he wants a life that's stationary? No.

No.

He wants to chase me. He's practically begging me to run right now. He's dying for some action.

Problem is, right now? I can't move, much less run. I put my hand on his chest, not intentionally. Because gravity is melting alongside me, my heart floating miles above my head, and if I don't touch him, I'll fall. Except that's not true, either, because touching him?

Makes me fall even more.

He opens his mouth to speak. "Ada—"

"Oh my god, shut up," I say, each word soft, each syllable pulling me closer to him, to his lips, until I crush my mouth against his, until I taste the way he says my name.

"Ahem."

I contemplate murdering stupid fucking Strom Fetor. Instead, I pull back at his stupid fucking voice and only *visualize* punching his stupid fucking face rather that actually following through on my heart's desire. Because *of course* it would be Strom Fucking Fetor that would interrupt me kissing Rian.

I glance at Rian, whose entire expression clearly says: *Okay, yes, you were right, I hate him too; we should have let him die in a fiery inferno of death.* I might be paraphrasing that look.

When Rian turns to the man, though, he's plastered on his professional mask.

"You've got a little something," Fetor says before Rian

can speak. He touches his own lips, a mirror to where a smear of red stains Rian's.

So, I'm getting a little sloppy. Who can blame me? Lip gloss looks good on Rian, anyway.

Rian licks the corner of his mouth, his tongue still tasting my kiss. "Can I help you?"

I open my reticule and retouch my lip gloss, using the tiny mirror on the cap to check my face. The stain and protective layer I put on before keeps the red where it's supposed to be; the gloss smeared on Rian's skin but stayed in the lines on mine.

Fetor smirks at Rian. "I was going to invite you to the afterparty at my estate, but I can see you have plans."

"No, I—" Rian starts, but Fetor cuts him off.

"I get it." Fetor holds his hands up, palms out, as if placating Rian. "I'd make the same call." He winks at me. "Thanks for the phone."

"Consider it payment to never have to see you again," I say brightly as I loop my arm through Rian's. "He's just walking me out now. If I can't seduce him, I'll send him to your little party."

"You can come, too," Fetor offers, speaking about five inches below my chin.

"I would rather evacuate myself from an airlock without a suit, giving myself over to the cold embrace of death," I say cheerily, smiling brilliantly.

Fetor laughs as if I'd told him a joke, but I'm already pulling Rian toward the exit, my heels clacking on the stone floor.

"So, I do actually trust you enough to believe that you're not working with the Jarra," Rian says as we maneuver around drunk rich people. "But I have to admit I'm a little surprised you didn't let Fetor's hover stage crash down in a blaze of glory."

I swallow down the distaste on my tongue. "Please, let us never speak of that again. I am mortally embarrassed to have missed that opportunity."

I feel Rian's pace slowing as we get closer to the big doors. The security has removed the scanners; they don't care what we leave with. Rian knew this would happen; he helped set up security. And even as we get closer to the exit, I can see the gears turning in his mind, wondering what I've been able to steal right out from under his nose.

Sure enough, he pulls me to a stop in the little alcove where the guards had watched the prepaid pretense of a protest play out. "I've trailed you all day," he says.

Except when you left me in Phoebe's hands or had your goons watch me, I think.

"And you've not even *attempted* to steal anything," Rian says. "At first, I thought it was that red Mission Control phone, but you just rejected going to Fetor's afterparty, and if you were going to steal the phone . . ." His brow creases as he tries to wrangle his mind around logical thought. "You said before the trick was to move something you couldn't steal. And you got Fetor to move the phone, but then you didn't care about going to his party . . ."

"I don't want to steal the phone," I say. Truth.

He looks like he wants to argue, but he's not sure which pieces to fit together to form the image in a jigsaw puzzle.

"Red phone, red herring." I giggle, then I lean over and touch the smear of my gloss still on Rian's lips. "Red stain."

His head bends close to mine conspiratorially as his shoulders shake with almost-silent laughter. "Fetor's face when he caught us," Rian gasps out, and I almost feel bad for him, because when the drunken levity of this night leaves him, I'm pretty sure he's going to be embarrassed about this. So, I kiss him again, an apology, and when I pull away, his eyes are dazed.

I tuck a lock of his disheveled hair behind his ear.

"You've not even attempted to steal anything," Rian says slowly, as if he has to pull every word through fog before he can focus on them. "You've not only committed no violence—"

"A record for me."

"—but you also prevented violence."

"I asked you not to remind me of that."

"I knew—I *knew*—you'd come tonight, though." Rian shakes his head again, not even aware that he is doing it, I think. Trying to clear his mind. His gaze focuses on my left ear. "You're missing an earring." He giggles, like there's been nothing funnier than my lost earring, then he sobers, a little frown line between his two usually sharp eyes, and I can almost see him questioning why he would find a missing earring funny.

We start walking through the big front doors out toward the steps. I veer Rian to the tread ramps to the sides. My feet are killing me in these heels, and he's already stumbling.

"I *knew* you were going to come tonight," Rian mutters, his voice wobbly when the ramp grips his feet and the rubber tread below starts moving him toward the street.

"And I did," I say. Despite the city lights, I can still spot some stars peeking through the night sky, silver clouds hiding the big moon, and the little one a sliver of a crescent, a sharp-edged bowl about to tip the stars out, letting them sprinkle down on us.

"But you didn't steal anything," Rian says, a hint of a whine in his voice.

I was right. This one *lives* for the chase.

Good thing I like running.

I pull him against me as the tread under our feet smoothly glides us around the curve of the ramp. "I told you," I whisper in his ear, reveling in the way my breath makes him unravel. "I only came here for you."

Okay, that's not entirely true, but he deserves my full attention right now. Besides? My other gamble? I'll have to wait a little while longer to see if that pays off.

But tonight? Tonight belongs to Rian. Me.

Us.

He pulls back, suspicion giving him a searing beam of light through the fogginess clouding his mind. "Why? To gain my trust? To deliver a message? From who?"

We step off the treads of the ramp, and I stumble a little on the hard concrete sidewalk. Dumb shoes.

"Can't a girl just want a romantic date?" I ask.

Above, at the top of the imposing white steps, a flash of red. Phoebe scans the departing crowd, her gown a fiery streak, the electric lights in her braided buns a demonic halo. I tip my face toward her, and when she notices Rian, me, us, she just nods and steps back into the museum.

"A date?" Rian laughs. "Maybe it's just the relief of all this being over . . ."

Or maybe it's the psychotropic drug in my lip gloss that I've been purposefully planting all over him, so strong that only the color seal on my lips keeps it from bleeding into my bloodstream, so powerful that I resisted chocolate-covered strawberries just to make sure I didn't risk coming under its intoxicating effects.

I steer him toward the corner and the ride I've already arranged. A good hunter, after all, knows not only how to secure her prey but how to transport it.

"Oh, Rian," I say gently, pouring him into the backseat of the rental self-drive. "This night is far from over."

17

Rian wakes up slowly, groggy. His gaze focuses on me, and a little smile carves into his lips. Oh, that does something to my heart. Oh, shit. This is going to be trouble.

His eyes widen, and he sits up in the bed, head whipping around.

"Where the fuck am I?" he asks. Realization zips through him like an electric shock. "Am I on your ship?" He's confused but not panicked, not yet. He knows—he must know—that my ship was docked not more than an hour away from the Museum of Intergalactic History. Whatever scheduled agenda he's got running through his head, he's probably figuring out how he many bullet points he can still cross off, depending on how long he was passed out.

"Welcome to the illustrious *Glory,*" I start, but he cuts me off.

"Am I in *your bed?*"

"You don't have to sound so ungrateful about it," I grumble. "There *is* only one bed on this ship."

"Did we— What did we do?" There's a manic edge to

his voice now. He's taking it all in—the narrow bed, his jacket crumpled on the floor, my change in clothes from an expensive gown to a serviceable (and comfortable) shirt and trousers.

"Don't worry," I say. "You snored through everything exciting, and I don't take advantage of drunk people. We got back to the docking bay, and you pretty much immediately just fell asleep. You're welcome, by the way. I slept in the cockpit."

Disorientation wars with panic inside him, that much is clear, but he also seems pretty relieved that he's safe and didn't do anything he'd regret. Which, fair. I'm going to make him work a little harder than this before I let him regret anything he'd do with me. Regrets are more fun when the choices they derive from are made intentionally.

"Wait, drunk?" Rian asks. Those razor eyes are wide awake now. "I wasn't drunk."

"Drunk on love?" I suggest.

"What did you do?" Accusation weighs his words down.

"Me?" If I had pearls, I'd clutch them.

"Ada," he says as he swings his legs over the side of the bed. Feet on the cold metal floor, grounding him, forcing him to focus, to wake up, to realize.

I roll my eyes and tap my lips with my finger. I watch as he looks at my lips, his gaze softening for just a moment. He remembers our kisses.

The first one, when Phoebe noted that no color came off on his skin.

His face pales.

The second one, with red so vivid that even Strom Fetor commented on it.

I reach in my pocket and grab the lip gloss. "Color seal to protect me from the effects," I say, tossing the tube to him.

He pulls out the wand, looking at the goopy contents. There's nothing in them to indicate that they're laced with a Gliese-Earth native plant commonly called "drunk sticks." The plant looks like a cross between aloe vera and snake plants: thick green stalks that point straight up. Squish the innards and rub them on your skin, and you become highly suggestible. Ingest even a little and you're walking loopy, cross-eyed and totally blackout drunk for several hours.

Rian's brow creases as he pulls the applicator out and sniffs the lip gloss. "Drunk sticks?" he guesses.

"Drunk sticks," I confirm.

"Ada, this shit's illegal," Rian says, firmly screwing the tube shut and tossing it back to me.

"Oh dear," I say flatly. "Illegal. Oh no."

Rian stands up, shaking his head. "What's even your end game with this? Fuck me, I thought you were coming to the gala to steal something and—"

"I did," I say. "I came to steal you."

He shoots me an exasperated look. You know, it's nice to see the façade breaking. I didn't like the way Rian acted at the party, all formal, corsage pinned down with an allegory and jacket buttoned up tight. But now he's letting his emotions show, even if his emotions are one hundred percent pissed off at me.

"You didn't have to stage such an elaborate . . . fiasco just to talk to me in private."

"*Fiasco*, nice."

"As you have pointed out *many times*," he adds through clenched teeth, "what you did at *Roundabout* wasn't technically illegal."

The best kind of legal: technical.

"You could have literally walked into my office and told me anything. Hell, you could have—"

He stops there, but I can see what he almost said. I could have approached him outside the office. I could be someone who has something more with him than business.

"Yes, but . . ." I say, trailing off, still half-thinking about what a talk with Rian White outside the office might be, wondering if he envisions a classy bar with expensive wine or an evening walk with twinkling city lights, or maybe his home. His home, like I've shown him mine. I would have been more polite about it, though. But I was raised better than he was; I try not to hold that against him.

"Anyway," I say, standing up. "Would you like a snack?"

"No!" Rian bellows. "I want to know what the fuck is going on!"

"Okay, fine." I roll my eyes again. "But I'm going to explain with a snack."

I head to the door, and Rian trudges behind me. I can hear him muttering under his breath, "The damn strawberries." I couldn't risk eating anything when I had the gloss on my lips. Our kiss was sloppy enough to make me reckless, but I was able to avoid ingesting any or getting much direct-skin contact from the sticky stuff.

Glory doesn't have a huge mess hall; it's mostly just a room with a reheater, a tank of recycler worms, and crates of ready-eats. And, of course, hot sauce on the table. "Yellow or red?" I ask, grabbing two of the boxes of ready-eats.

Rian makes a face that is, frankly, rude, because at least I've offered him some variety. I peel back the foil top of a red box and slurp some down. It's not exactly charity-gala fare, but it's better than the product of recycler worms, and the hot sauce perks me up a little.

"All right, what was so important that you had to kidnap me?" he asks.

"You're not a child."

"What?"

"Kidnapping. Napping kids. You're not a kid," I point out. Rian heaves a sigh from the very depths of his soul, so I figure I should let this one go. "Okay, fine. This all circles back to the *Roundabout*, which is ironic if you consider the name of that ship—"

"Ada."

"So, you mentioned before that while I stole the plans and the nanobot prototype from the salvage, I only delayed the government's process of creating them."

Rian nods.

I gulp down a little more of the red stuff. It has a label identifying it as beef replacement, and the picture on the crumpled-up foil shows a steak dinner, but this is nothing like that. I would have stocked up on better food, but even with the advance in funds on this job, I'm skint. "Did it not occur to you that I wasn't trying to stop the nanobot production?"

Rian's face crinkles as he processes that.

"Well, I mean, *I* wasn't trying to do anything but the job I was paid for," I continue. "But *they* knew better than to assume one theft would stop the whole machine of the government. The bill, as you pointed out, was passed. The Goliath was lumbering into motion."

"Then why—"

"For fuck's sake, Rian, just because you're good doesn't mean the government is. The government is a for-profit business that has to make the ledgers go from red to black. The more altruistic you think this nanobot production is, the more I question your intelligence."

That was a low blow, and I regret it the minute I say it. I could call Rian almost anything and he wouldn't care, but *stupid* crosses a line that actually insults him.

Still, though.

I wad up the empty ready-eat package. "Look, while you intended for the nanobots you're releasing on Earth to be beneficial to the climate, you had to hire out Fetor Tech to make them. And Strom Fetor's not exactly known for his giving nature."

"I know, but—"

"But you wrapped up this project in lots of legalese, I know; I read the bill."

"You read—"

"Yeah. The whole thing. I can read," I say, mildly insulted.

"I know you can. I would never call you dumb." He pauses, weighing his words. "In either sense of the word."

Fair. Also, a pointed blow against my insult. "Anyway, I know you think you safeguarded the whole thing. But you may know how to write a proposal or, I don't know, a memo, whatever you do all day, but you know jack shit about code."

He opens his mouth to protest, but he remembers the one bad mark on my public profile—I got pinned for hacking the European ad system to deliver anti-government messaging. And, more recently, I read the code from the

Jarra hacking in to the hover stage they'd set for a crash landing.

"Strom Fetor isn't a trillionaire because he gives things away, even for the government label."

"Of course not," Rian says, exasperated. "He was paid."

I snort. "Anyway, I looked at the code. I mean, my client did, too, but I wasn't going to just hand it over without looking at it myself. Planned obsolescence."

Rian's brow wrinkles in confusion, and even though I know he knows what those words mean, they're so far removed from the context of the illusion he's created around this program he can't figure it out.

"Planned obsolescence," I say again. "The nanobots are coded to malfunction after a certain threshold."

"Well, obviously, they can't work forever but—"

"Planned," I repeat more emphatically. "Planned. They *will*, without a doubt, stop working the way you want them to, and they'll start working the way Strom Fetor wants them to. See, it's like this." I don't have fancy holographics to illustrate my point, so I use my hands. "The nanobots are designed to go into Earth's water system, strip out the pollutants. It's actually a really clever design."

Rian nods; he knows all this. The microscopic bots are developed like a virus, attaching themselves to H_2O and attacking microplastics, carbon, sulfur dioxide, nitrogen oxides, and anything else that's negatively impacting the water cycle. It compartmentalizes the microscopic pollutant agents and eventually coalesces them into a slime-like matter that can easily be picked up by cleaner drones and then separated in recycling units. Like a virus, the nanobots will continue with a single-minded goal. And like a virus, it replicates itself.

Once released, it will never be able to be contained again.

Except, within a few years, they'll start hurting the environment rather than helping. It took some digging, but I found the code systemically embedded into the program, designed to be countered by more nanobots. Code that would require physical updates, a second program, just like this one.

The fact that *this* program happened in the first place is a marvel. A testament to people like Rian, people dedicated to fighting the good fight, getting bills passed, and scrounging up the funding needed for them to happen.

It's rare that sort of thing happens.

"Did you see the protest?" I ask him. Rian's still processing the information I gave him, the code I showed him on my data pad.

It takes him a moment to connect the thought. "The protestors outside the gala? They were paid by Strom, for the story."

"But the sentiment is real," I say. "Didn't you hear all the people who agreed with it? You're from Rigel-Earth; what do your parents think of the aid tax?"

His lips go hard, a thin white line around the pink.

"Everyone's fine with saving Earth as a concept, but when it comes to taxes, to action, to money?" I shake my head.

"We can reprogram the bots," Rian says darkly. "We can hire new outside sources to analyze the code and ensure they're not designed to fail."

"In a week?" Because that was the point of Strom Fetor's speech tonight, the grand closing ceremony of the gala. To announce to the galaxy that this was in motion, that it would not be stopped.

Pausing now would show the entire galaxy that Earth can't be saved. It jeopardizes the whole program; it gives protestors the footing they need to challenge it. It's not out of the question that they simply shut it down, but it's also not guaranteed that climate cleaners will recover if there's a public mark of shame on them.

Rian looks up at me, and I see panic in his eyes for a second time. First, it was because he thought he'd slept with me while blackout drunk. He thought he'd made a mistake. Now?

Now he knows he made a mistake with the nanobots, and he knows there's no time to fix it.

"Fortunately," I say, beaming at him, "I have a plan."

18

ou?" Rian asks, incredulous. "Or the people you work for?"

I shrug. Same difference. "The people who hired me suspected Fetor wasn't exactly an angel benefactor. So, they wrote some code that can correct the mistakes he purposefully made. Crypto-locked, of course, so it can't be overwritten."

Rian doesn't like this plan, I can tell. It's butting up against his own ignorances, his own blind spots.

I talk fast. "All it requires is an upload; think of it like a technical patch. It doesn't alter the nanobots in any way, but it does force them to continue the good programming without reverting to the bad. I could get technical, but—"

"But I wouldn't understand it."

I nod slowly, watching Rian's face. He can't know everything, and that grieves him.

He meets my eyes. "But you've looked at the code?"

I nod again.

"And you *know* it's good?" he asks.

"Yes." Quiet. Certain.

He's nodding now, mostly to himself, and I can see that he's willing to believe me.

Oh, that's going to make betraying him later hurt.

But for now? "I read every line of both codes," I say. "Fetor's version and my client's. And theirs is good. It's true. It does what you want, what we want. It will save Earth."

He looks me right in the eye, and he believes every single word I've said.

He *believes*.

In me.

Fuck.

"So, what do we do?" he asks.

We.

Oof.

"The plan from your side is too far in motion to stop now," I say. "And believe me, my side's been trying."

Rian frowns at that.

I count the list down with my fingers. "Allies have tried to hack in to the system and rewrite the code; they've contacted various people higher up than you to convince them to delay or at least more closely examine the program, and—"

"Wait," Rian interrupts. "You've contacted my superiors?"

"Not me personally," I say. "They brought me in when they figured that you were the highest person in a position of power who might be willing to listen to reason."

Rian's emphatically shaking his head now. "No, no, see, who did you—I mean your people—I mean, whoever. Who was contacted? Snyder? Turner? They would have done something, I know—"

"Look, all I know is that of the half dozen or so people who were contacted, at least half of them knew the code was corrupted and didn't care. And the other half either didn't believe the evidence or suspected something worse."

"Knew and didn't . . ."

"Shocking, but *some* politicians don't actually give a fuck about the people they're supposed to serve."

"But—"

"But Fetor has friends. And I'd bet *Glory* that at least some of them are on his payroll."

"That's corruption! I need names; I need to root this out—"

"You need to focus," I say gently. "And recognize that this is all coming down to you and what you can do to actually help others in this precise moment. Because even if you had the names of the people who stand to make a profit from this little scheme, there are others. Corrupt politicians in a government are like cockroaches in a kitchen. You can *never* get them all. And the ones you see are just the dumb ones that don't know where to run when the lights cut on." I stare at him, marveling. "You really have no idea how rare you are."

"Me?"

"Someone who both gives a damn and is willing to put forth effort for said damn." I shake myself back into the moment. "Bad analogy. Anyway, I can see why this is all coming down to you; that's all. That's a compliment, by the way."

He doesn't seem to care.

But really, it is kind of miraculous. The group I'm working for successfully spotted a problem, but they could never get it changed in a meaningful way without aid from someone on the inside. Someone like Rian.

"Why you?" Rian asks. "Why did they pick you to deliver this message to me?"

I shrug. "They figured I could get the job done."

He's quiet for a long moment, long enough to make me consider getting a yellow ready-eat, even if I need to ration them out a bit. I'll have no chance any time soon to restock.

Finally, Rian says, "I have to get back to my office."

"Your office on Rigel-Earth?" I ask.

He nods. "I can call the committee together, and we can come up with a reason to delay the launch—"

"That's not going to work," I say.

"Why not? I know it's not ideal, and any delay will cast everything in a negative light, and—"

"And Strom Fetor may be the galaxy's biggest, richest asshole, but he's not *entirely* stupid," I say. "You delay for any reason, and it's not just optics. If Fetor knows that his code is going to be overwritten, he'll just release his bots early."

"No, he can't . . ." Rian's voice trails off as his mind plays a picture of what I've suggested. Everything else aside, Fetor knows that nanobots are highly regulated for a reason, and that reason is that once microscopic robots are released, they're hard to contain. Scratch that; not hard, impossible. And these motherfuckers are designed to be even more so.

"The bots are already locked and loaded at Fetor's office on Sol-Earth, right?" I say, knowing the answer.

If Fetor gets word of delay, all he has to do is push the button. Oops, nanobots released. He can chalk it up to an accident or whatever; it doesn't matter.

He has the contract, the government approval, the bills to back him up.

Even if he did release the bots a little early, they've already been approved. And—*technically*—releasing them early wouldn't be illegal.

"Fuck," Rian mutters.

"See?" I say. "*That* is why I kidnapped you."

Rian frowns.

"We are going to have to break in to Fetor's offices," I say. "I've got the coding to update the nanobots. All we have to do is get in before they're released; I'll overwrite the code, and then—"

"*We,*" Rian says.

I nod. "We. I'm coming with you."

"You are not. I'm going to my office and will assemble a team of people I can trust, and— Why are you laughing?"

"You're not going to your office," I say, still chuckling.

"There are procedures to this sort of thing," Rian shoots back. "Yes, it will be . . . complicated. But I know I can— Stop laughing at me!"

I can't contain myself; I'm doubled over, howling as I stand up and head to the corridor. Rian follows. "Do you really think I would kidnap you for a conference meeting?" I say, heading toward the bridge. "Do you think I'd go to this much effort just to talk?"

I swing open the bulkhead door. The carbonglass windows of my ship's bridge show the cloudy interior of a portal passage. Rian's mouth drops open.

"We've been in a portal for three hours," I say. "We'll reach Sol-Earth with enough time to beat Fetor to the office, I hope. I need your clearance, of course, to get in the door, but once we're in, we're in. I'll replace the code, Fetor will never know the difference until it's too late, and crisis averted. Also, once that happens, I get paid."

Rian silently crosses the bridge. He puts his hand up to the carbonglass.

He thought we were still on Rigel-Earth.

We're already lightyears away.

Heading full speed on the path *I* set.

COMM LOG: #5O213-JLN
SENT: 4 STANDARD HOURS AGO, LOGGED IN SHIP SYSTEM
LOCAL SHIP IDENTIFIER: *GLORY*
INCOMING COMM IDENTIFIER: *UNKNOWN*
HIGHEST ENCRYPTION
TRANSLATED: CONFIRMED SECURE

UNKNOWN: What the FUCK.

GLORY: Who is this?

UNKNOWN: You know goddamn well who this is.

GLORY: . . .

UNKNOWN: What the actual fuck were you thinking???

UNKNOWN: It may shock you to know that, actually, a lot of people are really mad at me at any given time, so your rage doesn't really clear things up.

UNKNOWN: YOU KIDNAPPED HIM?!

GLORY: Oh, hi, Phoebe.

UNKNOWN: GIVE HIM BACK. WE NEED HIM.

GLORY: I didn't kidnap him so much as suggest he hitch a ride with me.

GLORY: He's fine, by the way.

UNKNOWN: Put him online.

GLORY: I can't. He's still sleeping.

UNKNOWN: You are WAY out of line, Lamarr.

GLORY: Let's keep this professional. You know comm lines are not secure.

GLORY: Asset acquired, en route to target location.

UNKNOWN: You were supposed to deliver a MESSAGE, not a person!

GLORY: So . . . I should charge extra for this service? I'll add it to the bill.

UNKNOWN: YOU SHOULD NOT HAVE LEFT RIGEL-EARTH AT ALL.

GLORY: Look, calm down. I'm delivering him to the location.

UNKNOWN: You were supposed to present him with information, convince him of the truth, and deliver him to ME.

UNKNOWN: That was the mission. You went rogue.

GLORY: Oh, that sounds really awesome. "Went rogue." But also . . . I feel like this is on you guys. You should have seen this coming.

UNKNOWN: Your absolute treachery? YEAH, WE SHOULD HAVE.

GLORY: Good, we agree!

GLORY: And hey, I'm not a traitor! I'm delivering the goods *personally*. Some people would pay extra for that service.

UNKNOWN: How dare you jeopardize the entire mission like this.

GLORY: Hey, I'm about to go into a portal, so I'll lose comms.

UNKNOWN: DO NOT LEAVE THIS SYSTEM.

GLORY: See you on Earth! :D

<<End Communication Sequence>>

Glory is now offline.

DEPARTMENT OF
INTERGALACTIC BIOTECHNOLOGY

SUBJECT: [BLANK]
MARKED: TOP SECRET
Highest level of encryption

From: Rian C. White, DoIBiTe
To: Phoebe Brücke, DoIBiTe

Phoebe,

~~The Person of Interest we had previously marked as a target has~~

~~I am currently being detained and need you to~~

~~After discovering the full extent of the prior mission, I have decided to~~

~~ADA FREAKING KIDNAPPED ME AND NOW WE ARE ALL IN THE SHIT~~

~~I am taking private transport to the location and would like to request~~[2] [3] [4] [5]

---

1 Fuck, I forgot no comms in portals.

2 I can't get a message out anyway. And anything I send after the comms are back online will be too late.

3 Oh my fuck, I have to trust Ada.

4 There's no other option.

5 Earth is doomed.

TRANSCRIPT ON RIAN WHITE'S PERSONAL DATA RECORDER

STATUS: Offline

NOTE 1: If all goes according to Ada's plan, we will have about three days before the planned nanobot release from Fetor Tech Industry's main building. It's *tight*—there will be no room for error.

The irony that I'm using a damned data recorder right now is not lost on me.

But it's talk to this little recorder or talk to her . . .

NOTE 2: I keep circling back to the red telephone.

After everything, she seemed *so* fucking interested in that red fucking telephone.

But she didn't make a move to steal it.

In fact, she made sure it ended up in Fetor's hands.

NOTE 3: She said she could steal something she couldn't otherwise get by getting it to change location. Did she kidnap me just to use me to get into Fetor's offices so she could *then* steal the damn phone?

NOTE 4: This can't possibly be about just a telephone.

But it *is* worth a lot of money to the right collectors . . .

No.

Maybe?

No.

. . . maybe.

NOTE 5: Fucking hell, there really is only one bed on this ship.

NOTE 6: It won't be long now before we reach Sol-Earth.

She's right. We have to reprogram the bots. I trust her enough to believe that much is true.

But whatever *other* play she's got going on? The real reason she needs to be *personally* inside the Fetor Tech building?

That is what I'm going to have to figure out and stop her from completing.

Somehow.

ACKNOWLEDGMENTS

This book is my kind of batshit. I threw everything I loved into it: heists and chaos and pretty dresses and saying the inside thoughts out loud and a little bit of social commentary and a little more chaos for fun. I am beyond grateful that my zaniest ideas were met with nothing but enthusiasm from the team behind this book.

Special thanks to my agent, Merrilee Heifetz, for not blinking an eye at this idea from the start. Gratitude also to Rebecca Eskildsen, who in addition to being awesome, also came up with the title. Both of these brilliant women's belief in this story is the reason you have it now.

The DAW team is remarkable and amazing, and I'd perform an intergalactic heist for them. Navah Wolfe knows exactly the right questions to ask to make Ada shine and be smarter than me. Madeline Goldberg is always on point and helpful, the steady calm a chaotic book needs. Laura Fitzgerald, Elena Stokes, and Brianna Robinson, thank you for your enthusiasm and help in ensuring Ada's flight path reaches as many readers as possible. Joshua Starr, thank you for helping with the myriad of complications my footnotes, scratch-outs, and random formatting introduces, and Elizabeth Koehler, thank you for managing the production of this book and so many others. Betsy Wollheim, you've created a legacy in DAW books, and I'm so honored to be a small part of it.

Wordsmith Workshops friends: you inspire me daily, and thanks for the mutual bullying needed to get work done! Patreon friends: thank you for the encouragement and love and belief in my words.

Special thanks to me, who always said "if you get stuck in writing, just blow some shit up," and then when I got stuck in writing, I was able to use my own advice (even if Ada stopped the actual big boom). Go, me!

To my family: thanks for not letting the house burn down while I hatched intergalactic heist plans. Love to my son, who thankfully won't read this book because he thinks it's a kissing book, but would absolutely be even more of an evil genius if he listened to Ada. My heart to my husband, who has worked hard to ensure my son doesn't take over the world, Pinky-and-the-Brain style.

Sorry for cussing even more in this one, Mom. I would promise not to do it again, but . . .